Melody leaves her one-note Midwestern life behind to join a new orchestra forming in the Big Easy. She falls head over heels in love with the concertmaster, Phillip, but his past comes back to haunt them both as his former lover, Chelsea, tries manipulation and sabotage to tear them apart. They must navigate the competitive New Orleans musical world and their own desires to discover if they can make beautiful music together. Can they find a way to live in harmony, or will there be only discord?

Melody's Crescendo
Copyright © 2019 Marie Howard
ISBN: 978-1-4874-2597-5
Cover art by Angela Waters

Published by eXtasy Books Inc or
Devine Destinies, an imprint of eXtasy Books Inc

Look for us online at:
www.eXtasybooks.com or www.devinedestinies.com

MELODY'S CRESCENDO LOVE NOTES #1

BY

MARIE HOWARD

Dedication

To my family and friends, who bring music to my life every single day.

CHAPTER ONE

A melancholy trumpet song filled the rooms of the shabby shotgun house. The music was as mournful as the air was damp, and a bead of sweat rolled down Melody Bell's face. She paused, flipping her head to dislodge the droplet. It flew a few feet and splashed against an unpacked cardboard box. Melody continued to play. The audition was tomorrow. She'd settle in afterward.

She swayed as she coaxed the music from her instrument. She tapped her bare foot on the floor, and her fingers moved the valves as if the horn were an extension of her own body. More of her curly hair escaped its bun with every shake of her head, and as the music crescendoed and flowed, her hair grew wilder. Her eyes were closed, every cell in her body vibrating with the music. Her mind, however, was wandering. As it did, the music changed. It became faster, more clipped, angrier.

Moving to New Orleans had been a spur of the moment decision. She was twenty-three and hungry to prove herself, with the ink barely dry on her Bachelor of Arts in Music Performance. When she heard about the new jazz orchestra forming in New Orleans, she dropped everything.

Including Aaron. Especially him.

Her brow furrowed when she thought about Aaron. The trumpet squeaked a sharp, wrong note. He had never supported her studies, encouraging her instead to drop out of university, take some classes in a trade, and become something practical like a nurse's aide.

"You can do music on the side, as a hobby," he'd said.

The longer she studied, the crueler he became.

"What if you fail?" he'd asked. "What if you're not good enough to make a living? Does that mean I just keep supporting us forever?"

The reality was he wasn't supporting them. She had taken out student loans to cover her share of the rent, and his when he was late with it, which was often. She bought groceries and paid their bills, and he'd continually offer commentary on his contributions to the household, and how that made them even.

She paid the electricity bill. He made a homemade laundry detergent that made all of her clothes smell like they'd been left out in a vat of room-temperature butter. She paid rent. He bought a new PlayStation and gaming chairs. During the breakup, she mentioned the discrepancy in their financial contributions to the household, and he called her a haranguing bitch who used too much toilet paper.

Her stomach churned at the thought of their last fight. She'd tried to keep her composure but had let it slip just a little. Her boxes were already in the mail to New Orleans. She was leaving, and she was finished with Aaron.

"You think everything you do is so perfect, don't you?" he had screamed at her.

"Don't shout," she'd said.

"I'm not shouting, you'll *know* when I'm shouting!" he shouted.

"I won't. I'm done with this." She stormed toward the door.

He stepped in front of her, faster than he'd ever moved, fueled by the quickness of rage. He slammed a hand against the door.

"You don't get to just leave!" he thundered. He gathered up a handful of her shirt in an angry fist. She was shocked at his sudden violence, afraid, and furious at him for being him and at herself for staying so long.

This is it. This is when I become a news clip about a woman killed by an enraged boyfriend.

She didn't know where it'd come from. It was like her knee had a mind of its own. It shot out and connected with his groin. He dropped to the floor in pain, groaning and clutching himself.

"You don't get to tell me what to do," she'd said, icily, and walked out the door.

Her music floated through the air, taking a sudden mournful turn at the memory. She hadn't meant to let things go on as long as they had, so long that they'd both started to hate each other and feel betrayed by everything the other did. They had been good together, once. Her heart broke all over again as she replayed their two years together. Canoeing on a lake, her squealing as he dripped cold lake water on her back. Playfully fighting over frozen yogurt. The impossibly long nights at the beginning of the relationship, when they stayed up too late talking about music theory, her favorite, and the strategy of first-person shooting games, his. They would sit, rapt, as the other talked until, at last, they fell into her bed, in love and completely wrong for each other.

Another bead of moisture made its way down her cheek. A tear this time.

Her trumpet raged, her lips burned as the music built into a frenzy. Her memories turned a corner from sad to furious, and her mind riffled through them, searching for some sense of justice. There he was, picking a fight before she left to perform in a concert. There he was, throwing out some sheet music that was taking up too much space on a shelf, according to him, and replacing it with three video games. Him sitting, sullen, shooting down an imaginary army onscreen and her dreams in reality. Their worst fight happened while he was playing that game and resulted in his best score ever. He channeled his frustration with her into the game. It paid off, in the game, not in their life together. She had wanted to build something with him, but he only wanted to have her, to keep her as she had been at twenty, like a ladybug preserved in amber. He wanted her to stay the same, forever. She would have if she could have, but that wasn't how life worked. He knew it, on some level, and it made him angry, all of that life not working out the way he wanted. He took it out on her and made sure she knew there was so much she could have done but hadn't.

She played more quietly, melancholy notes floating through the muggy air. She hoped he was happier, though she knew he wasn't. He wouldn't be. He couldn't be. As many times as he had told her that was her fault, it never had been. She was back in her apartment in Cleveland, packing up the few things she would take with her into a dozen cardboard boxes. He told her she couldn't make it on her own. She was being ridiculous, moving with no job lined up, moving without him, leaving her family, their friends. Those family and friends told her, with hints of trepidation and concern in their voices, to follow her dreams, that she was uniquely talented and would go on to do great things, but if she ever needed to come home, they'd be there for her.

She hoped she would never need that support or never go back tail between her legs, a failure, reduced to teaching music lessons to those few kids affluent enough to afford private tutelage. No, she wanted to perform, and she had to try this opportunity, an orchestra just getting started in one of the hearts of musical life in the country. She had to make it. She just had to.

One long, low tone rang through the narrow house and out into the New Orleans night. She was as ready for the audition as she'd ever be. It was time to get some rest.

She ran a cloth over her trumpet, the brass smooth and

lovely. Melody smiled. She played multiple instruments, of course, guitar, piano, flute, and a passable cello, but of all of them, the trumpet was her instrument.

That night, lying in front of a fan, sweating and dozing fitfully, she dreamed in a loose collection of memories, wishes, and situations she would have changed if she could. As she sweat through her thin tank top, sleepy and watching the moonlight gently illuminating her bedroom, her mind worked to make sense of her new life. Had she really left everyone and everything she knew?

Not everything. She fought her sleepiness. *I still have music.*

Chapter Two

"Tell me I'm bad," demanded Chelsea.

Phillip's breath stirred the hair on her neck as he reached around and groped her ample breasts. His hard cock strained against his pants, pushing against her taut buttocks. He ran his hand down her stomach and slipped it under her skirt. She was wet already and spun around to face him. He grabbed her chin in his hand and kissed her, hard. She leaned back against the piano and spread her legs around him. Chelsea reached for his zipper, her lips leaving his.

Phillip whispered into her ear. "You're so bad."

She grinned and knelt in front of him. He shuddered as she ran her tongue over the outline of him and stroked his shaft. He groaned and grabbed her hair by rough handfuls. Her mouth was so warm and slick. His heartbeat sped, and he let his head fall back. She took him into her mouth as far as she could, stroking the rest of him with a thin-fingered hand, caressing his balls and working his dick. He felt a twinge of disappointment when she stopped abruptly, the warmth of her mouth replaced by cool air.

Chelsea's strong suit had never been patience, nor modesty. She stood, hiked up her skirt, and peeled down her thong. She kicked it off one foot and wrapped her newly freed leg around Phillip. The smooth tip of his cock slid against her slick folds. Overcome with lust, he grabbed her hips and thrust into her. She gasped, then laughed a deep, throaty laugh that quickly turned into a moan. He drew back, teasing her, then thrust again. They leaned back against the piano, its

6

smooth finish steaming with the heat of their passion. He breathed faster, his hand tangling itself in her hair, tugging her head back. He pushed his lips roughly against hers, and she opened her mouth, letting his tongue slide in. His mouth stifled her moans. He moved faster, a pulse in his groin throbbing as he came closer to finishing. She tightened around him as she began to climax, her legs squeezing his hips. She threw back her head and shrieked in ecstasy. He clapped a hand over her mouth and filled her with a hot rush of his own ecstasy, a deep groan escaping his lips.

She stood still for a moment, his passion giving way to shame. He slid out of her, and she unwrapped her legs from around him.

"You really are bad," he said, seriously. "You're bad for me."

She glanced at him and smirked. "Seemed like it was pretty good for you."

He shook his head and buttoned his pants. "We have to stop this. Once the concerts start, this has to end. It's unprofessional."

"Sure, sure," she said, rolling her eyes. She bent to collect her thong and gave Phillip a full view of her perfect round ass.

He couldn't help but stare, entranced. He wondered, not for the first time if she might be a witch, her body some sort of gris-gris.

She wiggled into her underwear, smoothed down her skirt and strode out of the practice room with a swagger. He sat on the piano bench and rested his head in his hands. He hadn't meant to become so entangled with an orchestra member, much less one with so much instability and passion.

He spun himself around on the bench to face the piano. The sheet music was open, right where he had left off when Chelsea came into the room and unbuttoned her blouse. He inhaled sharply and flipped the pages back to the beginning. Beethoven's Sonata No. 8 Opus 13, the *Pathetique*. He knew the word didn't mean the same thing, but he did feel quite pathetic at the moment.

He played the opening notes, some gentle, some sudden and hard, then the run down the keys into the romantic melody. Phillip's long fingers danced across the keys. The music picked up. He played fast, furiously, all of his unfulfilled desires flowing out through his fingertips. He played and played, picking up speed, rocking with each stanza, the speed ebbing and flowing for twenty minutes until the final runs when his hands flew impossibly fast, then slammed to the last note. He sat still for a moment, breathing heavily, then shut the fallboard gently over the keys.

Chelsea sat outside the practice room, rubbing a soft cloth over the body of her cello. She smirked at him. "I thought the violin was your instrument," she said.

"I thought you said these rooms were soundproof." He gave her a pointed and scathing look.

The smile faded from her face, and he walked away. His head was held high, his frame erect with a military bearing he'd never earned from combat, but from years of structured days practicing music. His mentor was the brilliant and difficult Gustavo Miretti. One could not be a slacker and train under Miretti. His reputation was of impeccable musical perfection, forged in a fire of suffering. Rumor had it that Miretti's students were lucky to get five hours of sleep a night and only on the rare occasion they'd performed to his standards that day. Mostly, he was disappointed in their progress. His disappointment, far from discouraging his proteges, fueled them. They competed with each other, with themselves, and with the slow progress that prodigies and the gifted made after they had surpassed everyone else.

Phillip was a legend among Miretti aficionados after mastering not one but two instruments, but only ever spoke of his violin training. His polymath prowess was well known, and he was proficient on multiple instruments, but his mastery? Well, he kept that a tantalizing mystery. Miretti's students were mum on the subject, only confirming that Phillip had achieved two master's marks from Miretti. The class had been small, seven students, and they were all silent on the matter. Their eyes narrowed jealously when Phillip's name was mentioned, but there was nothing bad they could say about the man. He was a consummate professional, though prone to a bit of drink now and then, and, of course, he had a weakness for beautiful women.

The New Orleans classical musical community was abuzz with speculation about his musical prowess, and Chelsea's gentle ribbing had in fact been an attempt to confirm that piano was his second specialty.

His stride faltered a step. The practice rooms weren't totally soundproof, he knew that. As much as he knew about Chelsea, he had still believed her when she said they were. Was that her magic? Making him believe false truths? His gaze darted back to her nearly impossibly beautiful face. She was absorbed in polishing her cello, but he still had the feeling she was watching him closely. Like a predator. A chill crept down his spine. This had to end before things got out of hand.

CHAPTER THREE

M elody had left plenty early to be punctual to the audition and arrived with time to spare. There was a bench directly across from the hall where they were holding the auditions, and she sat with her trumpet case next to her. She compulsively reached out to touch it. Her gaze roved over the ornate building in front of her, all pillars and wrought iron, white paint, and bougainvillea. Munching thoughtfully on a beignet, she sipped some coffee and scalded the roof of her mouth. *Damn, I'll just play past the blister.*

It was a warm day, a Tuesday, and humid. The air was New Orleans slow, reminding the residents of the city to move at a Louisiana pace lest they sweat too much or laugh too little. Melody wanted to laugh, to join some of the groups of residents and tourists walking along the narrow sidewalks, chatting and cheerful. It seemed like nothing could get them down. She felt sour and rude in comparison.

On the walk to the hall, her instrument case seemed heavier. Maybe it was the heat, or her nerves were already exhausting her. *Get it together, Red.* The thought was hers, but the voice in her head was her mother's.

She was ten years old again, and her mother was helping her with her math homework. It was all she could do to keep fractions straight, much less multiply them. There they were, at her kitchen table, with two whole pages of fractions to multiply, courtesy Mr. Irchke. The tears had been in her eyes. She couldn't tell her mother Mr. Irchke had thrown an eraser at her, leaving a smudge of green, dry eraser marker on her cheek, and the kids had laughed at her at lunch, telling her she'd been shit on by a leprechaun. She couldn't tell her, either, that Mr. Irchke smelled like whiskey. She didn't even know what his smell was, just that he smelled strange and mean and scary, and he yelled an awful lot. Little did she know she'd have a whole year of his shenanigans, and it would take a decade to shake the feeling she was too dumb for math, but at that moment, her mother was exasperated. She'd said to her the thing that rang through her head when she was feeling weak and beaten. *Get it together, Red.*

As harsh as those words sounded, they were a kindness. Her mother suffered no fools, but she also told no lies. She said that phrase to steel and bolster Melody. She said it in a way that reminded Melody that there was someone who believed in her. That she was someone who was capable of getting it together. She wasn't broken. She wasn't dumb. She wasn't weak. She was her mom's Red. She missed her mom, so much.

She popped the rest of the beignet into her mouth, felt it scrape against her scorched palate. It was so delicious, perfectly fried and sugared, that she didn't even mind. She licked the sugar from her fingers and slurped the rest of her coffee. It had cooled enough to keep from burning her again, but she felt the acidic brew slap against the area of her mouth it had already damaged. It would be a few days before she could eat anything hot again.

Focus, Red.

She watched a tall thin woman walk through the double doors, rolling a cello case behind her. Her shadow was briefly visible through the glass, then disappeared. A young black man with a trombone case entered next. She peeked at her watch. 8:46. Not so early she'd appear to be overeager, but plenty of time to settle in and tune before the auditions at 9:30. She sipped more coffee.

The inside of her mouth ached, but she felt too nervous and excited to let it get her down. *This is what you trained for. No need for nerves. You're ready.* She exhaled sharply and stood, tossing her coffee cup and beignet napkin into the trash can nearby. She smoothed her black skirt. Her stomach flipped when she saw that she'd smeared powdered sugar along her thigh. She wiped it frantically, but the sugar stayed smudged into the fabric.

Panicked, she grabbed her case and rushed into the building. As the door clanged behind her, she continued to rub the powdered sugar. Distracted, she didn't see the man checking his watch in front of her and ran into him full-speed. Her elbow accidentally jabbed into his stomach. He gasped, wavy hair flopping in front of his eyes, the wind momentarily knocked from him. Melody was horrified. No powdered sugar disaster excused that much rudeness.

"Oh, my gosh, sir, I am so, *so* sorry!" she exclaimed.

He continued to gasp for air, rubbing his stomach.

"Oh, no, you're not a brass player, are you?"

He shook his head and smiled a lopsided grin through his pain.

"Violin," he gasped.

She was relieved that she hadn't completely ruined his audition by wrecking his breath support, though still distressed at the thought he'd be distracted.

"Are you okay? Do you need anything before the audition? Water? Can I get you some water?"

He shook his head again, smiling. "I'll be okay," he said.

She noticed the warmth in his brown eyes, then blushed when she realized just how handsome he was. Tall and broad, in a crisp white t-shirt and blue jeans that hugged his athletic legs. His arms were well muscled, his forearms twitching with the limber muscles of a committed string musician. His hair was dark and wavy, and his cheeks dimpled when he smiled. He was movie-star good looking and effortlessly charming.

Melody still had powdered sugar on her skirt.

"I'm so sorry, sir, but I have to find a washroom. Do you know where one is?"

Phillip smiled and pointed, still catching his breath. This lovely but sturdy young hopeful thanked him and hurried down the hallway. He watched her retreat, her small frame delicate but strong. Her hips swayed alluringly, and he found himself utterly distracted. He closed his eyes and shook his head. Phillip strolled toward the group practice room where the judging would take place. He rubbed his stomach idly. *Good thing they're blind auditions.*

Chelsea was already there, just inside the door, and smirked when she caught his eye. Her dimples deepened as he gave her a quick, surreptitious smile. God help him, but he just could not resist her, but for some reason, his thoughts turned to the redhead who had just body checked him in the hallway.

He walked toward his seat next to Anna, the other judge and general manager for the orchestra, and Francis, the conductor. Together, they'd be making the decisions about who would make the cut and in which chair they'd sit. A sheaf of papers sat on the table, clearly marked with numbers and letters at the top and a simple numerical ranking below. One through ten, in six categories, with a few blank lines at the bottom for notes. He nodded at Anna and Francis and settled in for the long day.

A row of room dividers blocked the auditioning musicians from view. They'd be able to see the three hopefuls as they walked in, but not where they sat or who was performing. It was the only fair way to audition since studies had come out in recent years that showed the bias of watching someone attractive perform. Phillip sighed.

Wasn't everyone more attractive when they played music?

Anna leaned toward him. "I heard you already booked our first performance?" she said.

He smiled and nodded.

"Yeah, over at the Beaux Reve bandshell next month, on the 30th," he said.

"Phillip!" she exclaimed. "Isn't that a little ambitious? It's less than two months away."

He grinned, her nervousness fueling his excitement. Maybe it wouldn't be perfect, but they'd make it work. They'd all decided to start this endeavor because of their love of performing, and when Edmund St. Claire agreed to fund the venture, well, it was settled. It didn't pay a whole lot, but it was enough to get by, and they were free to create their own performance schedule. St. Claire had given them carte blanche.

Phillip was ecstatic when Anna had called and told him the news. This orchestra was their baby. The two of them and Francis.

Francis was a grandfatherly figure, all unkempt white hair and a paunchy belly. He had taken Phillip under his wing after Phillip had finished his schooling. Not only did Phillip have the prestige of Miretti's approval, but he also had the psychological scars of his lessons. Francis understood. He'd studied under a similar mentor, but instead of making him hard-hearted, he'd softened and resolved to let his love of music be kinder. He was the leader that everyone followed out of adoration, not fear, and his reputation and fame had spread across the musical world.

Melody stood at the door to the practice hall and spotted Francis's mop of white hair. He was a major factor that had attracted her to audition for this newly minted orchestra. It wasn't just on a whim that she'd decided to pack up and leave her life behind, to say goodbye to the frigid winters and withering summers of Ohio and hello to the year-round warm and humid climate of New Orleans. Francis was known as someone whose passion for music never wavered, keeping his spirit youthful as his face and body aged.

She was tired, and at only twenty-three she was too young to be so tired. A voice in her head told her so, the little voice of reason nagging at her and reminding her that life wasn't just about making it work with one person out of habit, or paying bills, or even checking off boxes on her academic calendar. It was time to live for her, just her.

There she was, standing at the doorway to the practice hall. She peeked in with a thrill tempered with trepidation. Her heart fluttered as she saw the rows of seats in front of music stands, one of which she hoped would be hers. Her stomach clenched when she spotted the three chairs behind a set of screens. *Blind audition. That's smart.*

The tall dark-haired cellist she'd seen entering the building earlier knocked into her shoulder. "Excuse me," the woman said, irritably.

Melody's face reddened. "Oh, gosh, I'm so sorry, ma'am."

The woman's eyes narrowed. "Do not *ma'am* me, honey. We are contemporaries. And who says *gosh*, my dear? Do you think we are on a *farm*?"

Tears sprang to Melody's eyes. This was not how she'd imagined the day would start. There had been so much more of running into people and not nearly as much musician camaraderie as she'd hoped for.

The woman let out a huffy sigh. "It's fine, but I've got to get past. I need to tune. Are you auditioning as well?"

Melody nodded and smiled anxiously. She held up her instrument case. "Trumpet," she said proudly.

The woman looked at Melody's battered case for a long

moment. Melody could have sworn she actually sniffed at it with disdain but hoped it was just her nerves playing tricks. When the woman sharply turned on her heel and strode away, Melody was not so sure it was her imagination. She followed the chic woman into the room, feeling even more out of her element. She watched the delicate swan neck of the woman swivel and saw her gaze at the gentleman she had run into in the hallway. Melody watched as the handsome man chatted casually with a beautiful older woman with a jet-black bob, and one of her personal heroes, Francis Orchenbach-Keeves.

Melody realized with dismay that the man she'd run into was sitting, relaxed, with the other judges, holding a clipboard. He was a judge? Her heart skipped a beat. She turned to the woman deftly and gently removing her cello from its case. Melody was anxious, thoroughly intimidated, and could tell that the woman had taken an instant dislike to her, but her mother had raised her proper, dammit.

"Hi, I'm Melody," she said and extended her hand.

The cellist looked at the hand, then back up at Melody, as if Melody were offering her a handful of boiled oatmeal or room temperature fish. Reluctantly, she extended her hand and slid it into Melody's handshake. "Chelsea," she purred.

Melody squeezed Chelsea's delicate hand, but it remained limp and cool. Melody could feel the music in that hand, though, and whether or not Chelsea liked her was irrelevant. They could play together. She was sure of it. She smiled. Chelsea looked through her, then past her to the judges. As if Melody had disappeared, Chelsea dropped her hand, headed into the stands and took a seat slightly behind the judges.

Melody watched her, and her intuition chimed in. *Be careful of her.*

The auditorium filled up quickly. Melody watched a curious assortment of people enter, older and younger, and she struck up a pleasant conversation about New Orleans's food with a twenty-eight-year-old auto mechanic/baritone player. He showed her photos of his lovely wife and child, and Melody squealed at the picture of his chubby-cheeked baby.

Her attention wandered a bit, and her nerves tickled at the edges of her consciousness. This wasn't a social visit, after all. Her gaze ran over the first few rows of folks, then back to the judges.

With a jolt, she saw the handsome young judge she'd run into earlier staring at her. His eyes met hers. It was electrifying, even from this distance. She felt her cheeks warm. She smiled and was pleased to see his own cheeks redden as his gaze darted away.

Chapter Four

Chelsea settled in behind the judges and stared at the back of Phillip's neck. She tweaked the tuning keys of her cello strings and smoothed rosin on her bowstrings, all the while feeling the pull of the man sitting a few rows in front of her. *It's just sex.* She must have needed the reminder.

She looked at the smooth skin at the nape of his neck as it transitioned into dark stubble, then retreated under his thick hair. She remembered running her hand over that skin, through that hair, and her chin tilted upwards in silent pleasure. Her breath cooled the skin of her upper lip as she inhaled, sighing out warmer air, imagining that he felt her hot breath on that luscious hairline.

It's just sex.

She wanted to own every molecule of him. She wanted him to burn with wanting her, to be willing to do anything for her. To die for her. Her bow trembled in her hand.

It was just sex, she reminded herself again.

Chelsea watched his head swivel over to the mousy redhead multiple times. Each time it moved to her, Chelsea's hatred toward the girl ratcheted up. She looked corn fed. Average. Like she'd rolled off of a farm truck into Chelsea's beloved New Orleans. She stared at the girl's frizzy red hair.

God, she doesn't even have hair that belongs in New Orleans's weather. Who the hell says gosh?

For all her faults, though, Chelsea was at least aware of how unfair her thoughts were. The girl had been nothing but polite, but there was just something about her. She could tell.

Something that was going to make Chelsea's life harder, and Chelsea did not like it.

"Cellos!" called Francis. "To holding, please."

Chelsea filed toward the screens with six other cellists. There were six spots open, so this was a formality. *Starting the day easy. I'd have saved this for last when you're tired of making any decisions at all.*

They settled in with their cellos, added last minute rosin to their bows, and checked the tuning of their strings, then quieted. After a pause, they heard Phillip's confident voice.

"Cellist one, please," he said.

They went through their prepared pieces one by one. The judges scribbled notes. Chelsea played her best and was satisfied with the performance, though she was grateful it wasn't intensely competitive. If she was honest, two of the other cellists might give her a run for her money. She was sure she had outplayed them, though the judges were prone to subjectivity. She sized up the two cellists, a middle-aged man originally from Arkansas and a woman who was younger than her but who had a furious spark of rage and determination in her eyes that Chelsea recognized, appreciated and—if she was honest—feared.

"Thank you, cellists," said Phillip. "You are free to leave or stay for the other auditions."

Not a single person left.

The morning progressed through the strings and the percussion. During a lunch break, Melody and her auto mechanic friend went out for a quick bite of gumbo at a corner cafe he knew. Melody would have walked right past it, but its shabby sign hid a cafe of extraordinary warmth and cheer. The no-nonsense staff seemed just as willing to welcome Melody as to chastise her for not knowing what she wanted before she walked in the door. It helped that they brought her the most amazing gumbo Melody had ever had. The spicy stew warmed her heart, and she felt more ready than ever to play for the judges.

They returned to the practice hall and settled back in. Low brass was first, and it was a tougher decision for the judges. Almost all sounded great to Melody, but there was something a little stiff about Tuba #3, and Trombone #6 was truly awful. She snuck a peek at the judges while that trombonist was honking his way through a Cole Porter piece and had to stifle a titter. Anna's mouth hung open in abject horror. Francis sat stony-faced, looking as if the horn player had personally insulted him. Phillip rubbed his temples, wrinkling his forehead in the most alluring way. She was distracted by how supple his skin looked, but the mirth died in Melody's throat. This was a special opportunity for all of them, and she could see that Francis was taking the trombonist's lack of professionalism as an affront to their young organization. She turned back to the screens.

This was no laughing matter, she knew. New Orleans was still recovering after the hurricane that had wiped out so much of the city. This orchestra was forming to give musical opportunities to some of the people whose futures had been washed away. Sure, she was from another part of the country, but she wanted to be a part of rebuilding something in one of the nation's most fascinating cities. There was a rich culture here, a deep and complex history full of both tragedy and triumph. It was a far cry from her rural upbringing in Ohio, but one that she looked forward to embracing. The city was already in her blood. She could feel it.

"Trumpets!" called Anna.

Melody's heart leaped into her throat. *It's time. I can go ahead and be nervous until I step behind that screen. One, two, ready, go.*

Her knees shook slightly as she stood and walked toward the front of the room. By the time she'd reached the first row of chairs, she was feeling faint, but as she stepped behind the screen, a wave of calmness swept over her.

That's it. We're ready to go.

Twelve trumpet players were competing for eight spots. They snuck glances at each other, except for Melody. She clicked open her trumpet case and put on some white cloth gloves. She was focused on her instrument, blowing air through it, making sure there was no water in it, running her gloves over it to wipe away any smears on the glossy finish.

"It's a blind audition, honey. They ain't gonna mark you down for no smudges," said a middle-aged woman good-naturedly.

"I'll see them," said Melody with a reluctant smile.

The woman nodded and smiled back. "Good luck, honey," she whispered.

"You, too," Melody replied.

"Trumpet one," called Phillip.

First up was Renny, a stout black man from Treme whose accent was so thick Melody had a hard time understanding him when they'd chatted earlier, but he seemed friendly and pleasant. She hoped he'd make it, and his playing certainly didn't disappoint. He played with equal ease clear and bright tones, then with the down-and-dirty brass sound New Orleans was known for. He finished, and she smiled at him, but he stared at his feet as if he was unhappy with his performance. She patted his arm when he sat down next to her, and he smiled gratefully.

You were great! she mouthed silently.

Next was a lanky white banker from across the river, then the middle-aged woman, then two young men who weren't great players, then Melody.

She put her horn to her lips and blew one note to warm up. It rang through the room and pushed away her nervousness. She began to play.

Per the audition instructions, she played selections from

three pieces, a classical favorite, a modern orchestral piece, and finally, a section from her favorite song, *Do Whatcha Wanna* by Rebirth Brass Band. She had intended to only play the required 60-second selection, but when she finished, she realized she'd gone on through most of the song, stopping abruptly halfway through a phrase.

There was a pause before the room erupted into cheers and applause. She wasn't sure if it was because it was close to the end of the day, or if she'd actually blown the roof off of the place. After the anxiety and the slow crumbling of her life lately, she'd take a moment of applause. She looked over at Renny, who was grinning at her. He gave her an approving nod.

The last remaining auditions came and went, and at the end of the day, she walked out with her new friend, Renny.

"I think that went well," said Melody.

"Yeah, you right!" exclaimed Renny. "You fit right in here!"

Melody was relatively certain that was positive feedback. Renny clapped her on the back, his trumpet case swinging from his other hand.

"I see you roun', yeah?" he said.

Melody smiled and waved as he walked away. It would be a long two days before the results were posted, but Melody felt good about her audition. If the room's reaction was any indication, she was a shoo-in, but you never knew what the judges were looking for.

She stood forlorn at the sidewalk. It had been a long day, and she wasn't looking forward to the long bus ride back to her little house. She began to walk toward the bus stop when the handsome judge jogged across the street to her.

CHAPTER FIVE

"Hey! Hi!" he said. He reached out to shake her hand. "Phillip."

"Melody," she said, smiling. Their hands touched, and Melody's heart fluttered. She gasped, then blushed and hoped beyond hope that Phillip hadn't noticed. Her heart sank as he dropped her hand quickly.

He's beautiful. Enraptured, she had a sudden urge to reach out for him. His lashes were thick and dark around his eyes. The fringe gave them an almost deerlike quality, although there was a sensual promise in them she was sure you wouldn't see in the eyes of any innocent woodland creature.

"Glad you made it," he said.

Her heart leaped. *Does he mean I made it into the orchestra? No—they said they needed to go over their scores and discuss it for a few days.*

Of course, blind auditions. He couldn't possibly be about to tell *her* the results.

While she admired their commitment to fairness, she was anxious to get the results. She had, after all, packed up her entire life, moved two thousand miles, and signed a six-month lease on the little shotgun house. Granted, she had some savings, but it wasn't nearly enough to survive on without a little extra income. If she didn't make the orchestra, she had two options—look for work in The Big Easy, or go back to Ohio with her proverbial tail between her legs.

Phillip waved his fingers in front of her face. His nails were neat and clean, and his hands had a light dusting of dark brown hair on their backs. She wanted to twine her fingers into his, to draw his palms across her collarbone, and lower.

"Earth to Melody!" he laughed.

She recovered quickly, and she chuckled with him. "Sorry!" she said. "I'm a little fried after today."

"I hear that."

Words momentarily failed him. He was distracted by the electrical jolt of attraction he'd felt for her. Every line of her face was etched into his memory, as if she'd lived right there in front of him his whole life. She was so familiar, she might as well have been the Mona Lisa. He had never felt such a reaction to a woman. *Besotted. Is that what that word means?* She stared directly into his eyes with her huge, warm green eyes. Bold, he thought, his stomach quivering.

Is she the one? His mind rushed back to the smashing trumpet audition, the one where he, Francis, and Anna had exchanged a look and written FIRST on all of their cards without bothering to score anything. He stared at her lips, wondering if they had produced the music that stirred something in him so passionate that he loved it, feared it, and wanted to put it into song. He wondered how they'd look pursed into an embouchure or pressed into his in a passionate kiss. He smiled. She looked at him questioningly.

He opened his mouth to say something else when Chelsea burst out of the doors and strode confidently to them.

"Phillip!" she cried. "I'm absolutely famished. Shall we get some dinner?"

She wrapped her long-fingered hand around Phillip's arm. Melody took a step back, and Chelsea smiled. The moment was over.

"Well, it was nice to meet you, Phillip, Chelsea. I hope I'll see you both around," Melody said.

She turned on her heel and walked away with her head held high. Phillip watched her go with a mixture of longing and confusion. Who was this small redheaded woman who was so alluring?

Chelsea's fingers dug into his arm.

"Ow!" he yelped.

She giggled. "Just wanted to get your attention back on me," she purred.

She turned to face him directly and pushed her ample breasts against Phillip's torso. For the first time since they'd began their tryst, he was unmoved. He gently placed his hands on her shoulders and nudged her away.

"Not here," he murmured.

Her lower lip jutted out into a pout.

Something sour stirred in Chelsea's stomach. *It's just casual — nothing to be jealous of, because he's not yours.*

Her jealousy stayed exactly where it was, hovering at the edges of her consciousness, stubborn and upsetting.

Keep him. She couldn't ignore the growling voice inside her mind. *Do what you have to do. He is yours.*

CHAPTER SIX

Melody's phone rang two days later. She dropped the book she'd been reading on the floor. Her bookmark flew out, but she didn't mind. It was her sixth re-read of *Harry Potter and The Half-Blood Prince*. She wasn't upset at losing her place. She'd just start over.

"Hello, this is Melody Bell," she chirped, words run together and throat tight. *No breath support. Sheesh, what kind of brass player are you?*

"Hi there, Melody, this is Phillip Masters, from the St. Claire Symphony. We met the other day at your audition?"

Her heart beat faster, and she felt a flutter deep in her belly. She skipped from foot to foot and squeezed her fists. Holding the phone away from her head, she took a deep breath and let out a sigh. Calmed ever so slightly, she returned the phone to her ear.

"Of course. Thank you for calling, Phillip. How are you today?"

She could have slapped herself. *Get to the point – ask him about the audition! You know he's not calling for a social visit.*

Or is he?

Mind your own business.

Oh, my god, he's talking, what did he just say?

" . . . results, and we thought you'd all like to know right away. Congratulations, Melody Bell. Welcome to the St. Claire Symphony."

Keep yourself together. "Thank you very much, Phillip. I'm so pleased."

Pleased? She was downright ecstatic. She wanted to throw the phone away and shriek, run around the room, and skip. It took everything she had to hold the phone steady, or at least slightly steady. Her whole body was positively vibrating.

I'm so relieved. I'm so happy.

"I look forward to working with you," he said.

Was it just her imagination, or was there a *tone* in his voice? Some deep note of desire? Or was she hearing what she wanted to hear? Her breath quickened, and her lips parted. Something was happening, she was sure of it, but it might just be his handsomeness mixing up with her elation—the joy of her first gig as a professional musician.

"Me too," she said, grinning into the phone. "I look forward to working with you too."

"Good night, Melody," he said.

Every time he said her name, her knees felt like water. She sank back onto her chair.

"Good night, Phillip."

He settled the phone back into its cradle and leaned back in his leather office chair. Just talking to her had made his temperature rise, as well as made his pants feel too tight. She had an effect on him, this one. He wanted to call her back, ask her to meet him, to look at her perfect lips and her luscious red hair. His heart pounded, and his hand hovered over the phone.

As if he'd willed it into reality, the phone rang. He snapped it up, chest aching. "Hello, this is Phillip," he said.

Chelsea's laugh rang through the phone, crackling through her shoddy cell phone service. She must be on the bridge. There was never reception out there in the swamp.

"I know, honey, I just called you. I'm on my way, I'll be there in . . ."

The phone cut out. Silence rang loudly through the

receiver. He slammed the phone down, inexplicably angry. He hadn't invited Chelsea. Why was she assuming he was free?

It was Friday, he remembered. They had a standing date, if you could call it that, on Fridays. They met at his house and stayed in. His groin was throbbing, and he couldn't stop thinking of the redheaded trumpet player. *Melody. What a perfect name for her.*

The doorbell rang, and he rushed to the door. Chelsea stood there in a sleek charcoal gray trench coat. Her black stockings clung to her legs as she clicked through the doorway in her delicate and fierce looking patent leather stilettos. She flipped her long dark hair over her shoulder and pursed her red lips. She knew her effect on men and enjoyed it.

Phillip shrugged off his jacket. The second it dropped from his hands, he grabbed Chelsea's shoulders and kissed her, forcing his tongue between her lips. He tasted her red lipstick. She parted her lips and sighed. Her hands undid the belt of her coat, and she slid it from her bare shoulders. Underneath it, she wore a braless corset. Her breasts stood pert above the delicate boning and lace. A row of laces drew Phillip's focus down, past her navel, to the frilly garter belt that held up her stockings, framing her exposed pussy, waxed bare and inviting Phillip in.

He ran his hands over her smooth shoulders and under her perfect breasts. Her nipples hardened, and he rubbed his thumbs over them. She gasped and grabbed the front of his belt. He roughly tore at the front of his shirt, some of the buttons coming undone and others flying off the shirt entirely. Still kissing passionately, they staggered to the settee in his sitting room.

She shoved him onto the cushions, and hungry, he looked at her. She unbuckled his belt and unzipped his pants. He sprang free, harder than he had ever been.

Chelsea smiled. "I guess you like my new corset," she said and slipped him into her mouth.

He groaned as her tongue worked along his shaft. She moaned, and the vibration of it made him shudder. He ran his hands through her hair and gently guided her up. She grinned. He grabbed her hips, and she straddled him. He groaned again as she lowered herself onto him, taking his hard length into her warm wetness. He thrust into her, and she moaned loudly. Together, they found a ferocious rhythm that grew in intensity until, both gasping and shuddering, they came, hard.

She gently rose off him, leaving him feeling exposed.

"Dang," she drawled. "I guess I shoulda brought a shirt."

He smiled. "You can use this one, but it doesn't button anymore."

They laughed. She kicked off her shoes and put on his ruined shirt. She looked oddly at home in her corset and button-down, barefoot in stockings. He wondered what would happen when this ended. She'd obviously made the cut for the orchestra, but could they continue this tryst with the symphony becoming a reality?

It had been fun, of course, but it was long overdue to have *that conversation*. He cared about Chelsea, but he didn't see a future with her. She didn't see a future with him, either. While he thought she might care about him, she was not the type of woman whose caring for a man ever lasted very long.

Chelsea had had a hard life. Because of that, she'd become a hard woman. Phillip watched her pad into the kitchen and thought of the first time he'd seen her, sneaking out of his college suitemate's dorm room. Well, not sneaking, exactly. Strutting might be a more appropriate word. His suitemate was the son of a famous lumber baron, and Chelsea had gone on a single date with him. He talked about her incessantly for five months afterward. He pined, moaned, and cried.

Eventually, Phillip had tracked her down at the women's rowing tournament and begged her to see the lumber heir one more time, even if was just to let him down gently.

She had come to their shared living room, kissed Phillip on the cheek, then stripped off her clothes for his suitemate. Phillip left the room before her red brassiere hit the floor, but on his way out the door, he took note of both her spectacular breasts and the look of rapture on his roommate's face. He vowed to never, ever become emotionally involved with Chelsea Carr. From that day forward, until very recently, he hadn't. They had occasional casual sex over the years, but it had always been lighthearted and fun. The past few weeks, though, Phillip sensed something changing. Chelsea seemed sad, not her usual cheerfully wonton and brazen self. There was something more serious in her eyes when they met.

He knew they'd have to address it eventually. He leaned back onto the couch, and Melody's face floated into his mind's eye. *Maybe sooner than eventually.*

Chapter Seven

Two weeks passed. Chelsea led the cellos with a sharp tongue and devotion to perfection. Melody emerged as a leader of the trumpets, as well as the entire brass section. Her humor and commitment to the organization inspired hard work in the orchestra. Phillip stayed busy as concertmaster and co-founder. His hands were quite full.

During one of Chelsea's late-night house calls, as she pulled on her skintight blue jeans and zipped her fierce boots one night, she asked him directly, "Who is she?"

"What . . . what do you mean?" he stammered.

Chelsea laughed, not entirely kindly. She kicked her feet up onto his settee. Then the jealousy at the fringes of her mind flooded in. "The woman who is keeping your mind off of me, when I'm right here in front of you."

Her fingers toyed with the buttons on her blouse, idly undid the top, then second, then third. The fabric slid open, exposing her lacy bra and curve of her breasts. Phillip didn't even glance at her cleavage. She pouted and sat upright, quickly redoing her buttons.

"See?" she said, trying to mask her embarrassment. *What the hell, Chelsea? Keep it casual.*

"I . . . I don't know. I've just been so busy," he said, looking at the wall.

Chelsea frowned. She was right, there was someone else. Some-redheaded-one else, she'd be willing to wager.

"Is it the trumpet strumpet?" she asked, forcing her tone to be upbeat and teasing.

A hint of redness crept over Phillip's cheeks. Chelsea felt a lump in her throat. It *was* her.

"Trumpet strumpet? That's pretty clever, Chels," he said and turned his brown eyes her way.

She looked at her shoes. She couldn't meet his gaze. He was confident and calm, and she was the one breaking the terms of their relationship. *No emotions*, they'd promised each other. She swallowed hard.

He noticed. "Chelsea," he said, gently. He reached his hand toward her shoulder.

She stood abruptly. "I'll see you at rehearsal tomorrow," she said and stormed out the door.

This isn't good.

Melody and Renny strolled down the cobbled avenue side-by-side, laughing around mouthfuls of beignets and clutching their intensely hot coffee. She'd learned to wait before sipping the drink, lest she burn her mouth and have a miserable few days of practice. She and Renny had become fast friends after the auditions. She loved his quick humor, thick accent, and adoration for New Orleans, and he said he enjoyed Melody's easy laugh and endless questions about The Big Easy. One night, they'd gone on a Haunted New Orleans tour, and Renny had whispered the tragic true stories behind the sensationalized accounts the tour guide shouted through the bus loudspeaker. Afterward, they sat at a wrought iron cafe table on a cobblestone street and had cold fruity cocktails and watched the intriguing crowds of New Orleans walk past.

"This is a beautiful and sad city," she said.

He raised his glass of pink booze. "Yeah, you right," he said. "No place other like it in the worl'."

Melody smiled a melancholy smile. "It's a lot like life, isn't it?" she said. "Beautiful and sad. Full of joys and full of tragedies."

"It's all part o' life. You got t'take the good witha bad. Can't know the high notes if you can't play the low too, yeah?"

"Unless you play piccolo," she mumbled.

He threw back his head and laughed.

She watched a beautiful woman weave through the crowd and trip. She fell into the arms of a man who was clearly caught off guard. The two stared at each other for a moment, then she slipped her arms around his shoulders and kissed him on the lips. The two embraced, entwined, his hands running through her hair. They paused, staring into each other's eyes. Then she put a hand on his cheek, smiled, and walked away.

Melody smiled and pointed. "You saw that, right?" she asked Renny.

Renny was silent. Melody turned to him, but he was distracted by something in the distance.

"Renny?" she asked.

He looked at her, eyes wide. "How'd it get so late? We should go," he said. "It's gonna be a long day at practice tomorrow."

"Oh," Melody said, disappointed. She had hoped to stay out a little later, but Renny was right. They slurped the last of their drinks through their straws as they stood, walking a little unsteady as they left the table.

In the crowd behind them, Chelsea stared at them, glaring furiously. She had just emerged from a store festooned with voodoo dolls, dried herbs, and burning candles. In her hand was a paper bag. As she watched Melody's curls bob through the crowd, Chelsea tightened her grip on the bag until her knuckles were white.

The next day at practice, Melody was in an exceptional mood. She led the trumpets in a chorus of *Happy Birthday* sung to the second-to-last chair trombone player, then cracked mostly groan-inducing jokes during their breaks.

"Hey, Renny, how do you get a hold of a low brass player? You-phone-ee-'em!"

That earned a groan from the entire brass. Chelsea spun in her chair and held a finger to her lips, glaring furiously. Her other hand toyed with a leather strap around her neck. Melody's heart clenched when she saw Chelsea's enraged face. She sank back into her chair and sat quietly the rest of rehearsal. Though she knew Chelsea was right to rein in the shenanigans, her feelings were still hurt.

She squeaked a decidedly wrong note, and Francis halted the piece. He stared at her for a moment, then said simply, "Do better, Melody."

She thought of her parents, scolding her as a child for being too rambunctious in church. It was the exact same feeling. An overwhelming wave of discomfort washed over her. She suddenly felt unwelcomed in this new city, that perhaps she'd made a mistake moving here. She glanced around the room. People still chatted in pairs and trios, though nobody seemed to notice her sudden silence. Would anyone notice if she wasn't there? She blinked back tears, staring at her sheet music until she felt someone's eyes on her. She looked around the room, and her gaze met Phillip's.

Her body responded to his attention, warming and softening. His gaze felt like stepping into a warm bathtub. She smiled, and when he smiled back, her heart leaped. The rest of the room faded into the background. She felt so connected to Phillip, like she could float out of her chair and fly right to him, as if he was a magnet and she were made of metal. She felt it so strongly it didn't matter to her if she was being silly. *God, does he feel this too? He must.*

He had been sneaking glances at her all day, unable to take his eyes from her halo of red curls and the freckles sprinkled across her nose. Even across the room, he spotted details of her face, plucking awareness of each one like roses from a bouquet. Freckles, hair, dimple, crinkles around her eyes when she cracked a joke, a slight gap in her front teeth. Each detail made him pause and appreciate being alive. He'd never felt that way before, so enraptured and enchanted. He played their few conversations over and over in his head, seeking any hint of interest from her, but he'd found none. It didn't matter. He was obsessed. She was the first face that came into his mind in the morning when he woke. He imagined her red curls when he saw the morning sun hitting the bougainvillea, her green eyes in the ivy pouring over his neighbor's walls. He had retreated into a secret garden of immediate attraction, quietly examining this new, unexpected treasure.

Chelsea sensed his distance. That was how she knew for certain she'd broken the rules of their causal affair. She wasn't supposed to feel anything but unbridled lust and fierce orgasms. She had those, but she also experienced a sense of possession. A sense of entitlement, yes. He owed her some respect. He owed her just a little bit of composure and a clean break, but that wasn't what she wanted. What she wanted was for him to adore her and only her. She glanced back at Melody, the little moppet laughing and making jokes like she wasn't ruining Chelsea's perfect romance. She snapped at her and shushed her, then felt a twinge of regret. Her thoughts were entirely unwarranted, and she needed to control them. Better yet, she could control the situation. Her hand moved again to the leather strap around her neck, jostling the talisman she'd bought in the most legitimate-seeming Vodoun shop she could find. She stole a glance at Phillip and wondered about the best way to refocus his attention on her. An idea began to sprout in her mind, one way she might be able to secure his affections for years to come.

After practice, Melody nearly ran out of the building, mortified by both Chelsea's admonishment and her own unprofessional actions. *Stupid, Melody, stupid! Recovery is the key to performance. This is your chance to be taken seriously, and you're blowing it!*

Her vision swam as tears ran down her cheeks. Her head lowered, she rushed toward the bus stop where she sat on the bench. Her sniffles echoed off of the plexiglass around her. It was hot and humid, and she felt like a fool.

Footsteps grew louder as someone approached. She stared resolutely at the pavement in front of her, until a pair of well-worn shoes strode into view. She looked up into Phillip's beautiful dark brown eyes. He stared into hers, and without a word, he extended his hand to her. Her heart pounding, she took it.

He drew her to her feet and wrapped her in a gentle embrace. She slid her arms around his torso. His breathing was steady and deep, and she felt safer than she ever had in her entire life. Like a dam had burst within her, she sobbed into his soft cotton shirt. He rubbed her back with his palm, and with every movement, she felt warmth trailing behind his moving hand.

When her sobs subsided, she clung to him, breathing in his warm, spicy smell. There was a tiny hint of cologne, but the scent of his body alone was intoxicating. Melody became aware of his whole body, his broad shoulders, and taut stomach. She pressed against his athletic legs and, as if she was magnetically drawn to it, a bulge in his pants. A sigh escaped her lips, and he smiled. He put one of his large, strong hands on her cheek and drew her face toward his. Their gazes locked. She thought she might faint.

"We make emotion for a living," he said. "It can overwhelm us sometimes."

She said nothing, enraptured by his handsome face. She drank in his features, his strong jaw, and sharp nose. His dark and perfect eyebrows and, in the late afternoon, a shadow of dark stubble along that perfect jaw.

She tilted her mouth toward his. Like the slow and undeniable rise of the sun, his moved toward hers. When their lips met, the world faded into nothing. She had never felt anything like it before. His hand held her cheek, still wet with tears, and he kissed her salty lips. She melted into his arms. They tightened around her, just as her knees went weak.

A minute passed or an hour. Their lips parted, and the sound of crickets, traffic, and New Orleans rushed back at them. They stared at each other, silent. The world was a different place than the one they'd left as their kiss began.

"Melody," said Phillip, his voice thick with emotion. "Can I buy you dinner?"

"I would like that." The little salad she had waiting for her in her bare kitchen didn't even cross her mind. She was so entranced by this handsome man who had changed her world with just a kiss. "I would like that very much."

They went to a diner, and over hush puppies and the finest etouffee Melody had ever had, Phillip told Melody stories that delighted her and touched her heart in utterly unexpected ways. They talked at long lengths about their pasts. His, losing his parents to illness early in his life and moving into a renowned musical boarding school. Hers, an upbringing so prosaic that her brushes with danger included riding her bike down the neighborhood hill on a dare and flashlight Morse code after midnight to her best friend and neighbor. They spoke about their loves, their losses, and their hopes and dreams.

"I always wanted to live in New Orleans," said Melody.

"What made you want to move here?" asked Phillip.

Melody stirred her sweet tea with a straw and stared across the table at him. His foot was next to hers, and she let her ankle rest against his. He smiled. In the distance, a saxophone played.

"The music. The food. The people. It seemed more like home than Ohio."

"Had you been here before?"

She smiled, and Phillip reached a hand across the table. She took it gratefully. Her stomach fluttered. "Nope, but it sure does feel like home now."

He grinned. "I'm glad you're here, Melody Bell."

Hearing her full name from his beautiful lips made her heart beat faster. She wanted to press herself against him again, to do nothing for the rest of her life except kiss Phillip Masters, draw him into her, take him into her so completely that the world would never be the same.

The waiter brought the check, and Melody reached for her purse. Phillip waved a hand at her.

"C'mon now, Yankee, you know I can't let you do that."

She laughed. Her smile lit the cafe, and her laughter sent waves of cool delight down Phillip's spine. Was it too soon to be in love with this woman? The waitress came and went, then came again to mention that the cafe would be closing in a few minutes.

Melody glanced at her phone. "Oh, no, it's nearly midnight! Well, it's not even that it's late. It's that rehearsal is so early tomorrow."

Phillip never wanted to spend a second away from her but knew she was right. He also knew if they went home together, there would be no rest for either of them. He stood. "Can I give you a lift home?

She reached for his hand. "I would love that."

The word love from her lips made his knees weak. They walked to his car in silence. Melody stared curiously at him when he stopped at a sleek black Audi parked on a quiet side street. He opened the door for her. She slid in and ran a hand over the polished wood of the dashboard.

Phillip's body reacted as if she'd slid her hand over him. He eased himself into the driver's seat and started the car.

Melody leaned toward him, and before he knew it, they were wrapped around each other. His hands were entangled in her soft curls, his tongue deep in her mouth. *Too fast? No, just right.* He reclined the seat. She unzipped his pants and tugged downwards. His throbbing erection sprang free, and she wrapped a hand around his shaft. He moaned as she straddled him and rubbed herself against him. He could feel her wetness through her thin cotton panties.

He reached for her, slid his hand into her panties, and gently parted her wet lips. He ran a finger along her delicate moisture, and she gasped. She rocked her hips downward, onto his fingers, and he happily slid two into her. She moaned, and shaking, he slid in a third, gently stroking her clitoris with his thumb.

She changed her position, drawing herself closer to his hardness. Her warmth hovered over him, calling to some primal urge. He drew his hand from her and pulled her panties to the side. She slid down onto him. He groaned, and she grinned. She rocked her hips and worked him deeply inside herself, squeezing him with all her muscles. He gritted his teeth and fought to hold back his orgasm.

She angled herself, stroking his tip her against her g-spot. Her breath came faster and faster, then she moaned louder and louder until she cried out, and Phillip put his hand over her mouth to muffle the noise as she came

Feeling her shudder and tighten was too much for Phillip. He came in a hot rush with a cry of his own. They stayed still for a moment, panting, staring deeply into each other's eyes.

"Um," she said.

"Yes," he said.

She lifted herself, and he slid out of her, spent. She moved back to the passenger seat and adjusted her panties.

"That's not the kind of ride home I usually accept from strange men," Melody teased.

"I don't give rides to just anyone," he said, smiling.

Melody laughed, and Phillip decided it would be his new life's mission to bring that laugh into the world as much as he possibly could. It warmed his heart.

He adjusted the seat and adjusted himself, zipping his pants and turning on the headlights.

He couldn't take his gaze off her. She was impossibly beautiful in the dim light of the streetlamps through the tinted windows. Her skin glowed, and her hair curled in multiple directions, begging for his fingers to touch it, smooth it, muss it up again.

"Can I get a ride home after practice tomorrow night?" she asked.

He looked out the windshield and grinned a charming lopsided grin.

"Melody, my dear, how about a ride *to* practice tomorrow?"

She laughed and took his hand, and they drove off into the New Orleans night toward his house.

CHAPTER EIGHT

The next morning, Melody awoke to the first hints of dawn glowing through the window. She was momentarily confused, then saw Phillip's face just inches from hers, smiling in his sleep. He mumbled something unintelligible, then rolled onto his side and slung an arm over her, his naked skin warm against hers. She cuddled closer to him, the cool air tickling her bare skin. She ran fingers over his chest, marveling at his tanned skin and strong muscles. He hardened against her leg, and she moved smoothly to him, parting her legs and hooking one around his hip. She rolled onto her back, easing him with her.

He was still half asleep as he entered her. She gasped, sore from the night before, but she was throbbing with more than just overexertion. Phillip was large, and she wasn't used to the level of passion he brought out in her. He swayed his hips gently in slow love, easing himself in and out of her. She sighed as he did, her sighs turning to moans.

Awake, Phillip smiled down at Melody. He cradled her cheek in his hand. She tilted her head up, and he kissed her, softly. He slid his hand up her torso, gliding his hand over her breasts. Her nipples were throbbing, and he ran a thumb over them. She moaned, and her legs squeezed his hips.

They moved together, his thrusts becoming stronger, surer. Every muscle tightened, and she stifled her moans by taking the skin of Phillip's strong shoulder between her teeth. A pressure built in her pelvis until waves of liquid heat washed over her body. Melody shuddered and cried out, and Phillip's muscles strained against her. Melody's hips rose up to meet his one last time, and he moaned loudly, once, and cried out.

"Oh, god, Melody!"

She laid beneath him, panting, her skin beading with sweat.

Phillip relaxed over her, his weight comforting, and kissed her gently.

"Good morning, Phillip," she said with a smile.

"Good morning, Melody," he said.

He rolled over, and she wiped the sweat from her brow. He stood and walked toward the bathroom. The dim dawn light glinted on his damp skin, every muscle of his toned body perfectly highlighted by the glow. She watched him stride across the room and smiled, drunk on her attraction to him. He looked over his perfectly sculpted shoulder sporting a bit of a red mark from her teeth and smiled at her. He continued into the bathroom.

Melody heard the shower come on. She curled herself into a small ball, hugging her own bare body, sore and satisfied.

Phillip stood under the hot water and rinsed. He hummed to himself, a cheerful tune. He ran a soapy cloth over his skin, sudsing his face, and jumped when the shower door opened. A pair of delicate hands took the washcloth from him, and he allowed Melody to run it over his arms, his back, the curve of his buttocks. He let the water wash over his face, then turned to her. He gathered her in his soapy arms and kissed her, a chaste kiss, heavy with emotion. He blinked his eyes open and gazed at her lovingly. She smiled back at him, every cell of her body radiating joy.

He took the cloth back from her and gently ran it over her bare shoulders, down her alabaster breasts, and over her rosy pink nipples. They drank in the sight of each other, the first time they'd taken the time to really see each other. He sudsed the flat expanse of her stomach, curved around each hip, and with great care, the copper curls above her nether lips. She sighed when he ran the cloth there.

He lowered himself to his knees and guided Melody to the wall of the shower. He ran his hand from her ankle to her knee, behind her thigh, and lifted her leg over his shoulder. He ran his other hand up her other leg and gently parted her damp, copper curls and lips. She opened like a flower, the bud of her clitoris pink and inviting. He kissed the inside of her elevated thigh and felt her quiver. He kissed higher, working his way toward her exposed center as the warm water cascaded over them. He kissed her where her legs met and gently worked his tongue between her folds. She moaned.

He ran his tongue over her throbbing clitoris and tasted the salty wetness of her. As she arched against his face, he slid two fingers into her and gently worked them in and out. She rocked against his hand, each flick of his tongue bringing her closer to ecstasy. He licked and fondled her, his pace following hers until she gasped and shuddered, and a new wetness ran down Phillip's face.

He gently guided her leg from his shoulder and put her foot on the floor of the shower. She leaned against the tile, gasping for air.

Phillip grinned. "Time for practice!" he said.

Melody giggled, and, after her knees stopped shaking, finished rinsing herself off.

Chelsea stared at herself in the mirror over the sink. Her makeup was immaculate, her hair glossy and perfect. She smoothed her hair anyway and tilted her chin side to side. Reassured that she looked good, she turned to leave the bathroom. Just then, the door flew open, and Melody traipsed in.

Chelsea froze, a sudden wave of rage paralyzing her. Melody smiled at her, and Chelsea congratulated herself on not slapping the younger woman. With what seemed like, to her, superhuman strength and composure, she walked out of the bathroom with her head held high.

Chelsea strode down the hallway thinking about the cheerful redheaded girl. *Farmgirl. Podunk flyover hayseed, coming to my city to play my music? Making eyes at my man?*

She stopped short before the practice room. Her eyes narrowed. Through the window, she saw Phillip settling into his seat. He was positively glowing. Something was going on. *He's not yours. He never was, and he never will be.*

From somewhere deep inside her, somewhere buried so far inside she pretended it wasn't there at all, another thought flashed. *He could be, if you try, and he should be, don't you think?*

She stared at his dark, wavy hair and broad shoulders. She remembered being pressed against his body, shrieking as he brought her pleasure she'd never known. That had to be all the sign she needed, right? He was hers. She just needed to remind him before he got too distracted.

But the two of you agreed, said the rational voice.

Shut up, said the darker one. *He's yours.*

Chelsea tossed her hair over her shoulder and strode into the room. Two of the low brass players looked up and smiled at her, but she didn't even look their way. Phillip also looked at her, but she didn't meet his eyes right away. She rolled her cello case to her chair and popped the clasps, the familiar smell of wood and rosin soothing her nerves and strengthening her resolve. She was Chelsea Carr, dammit, and nobody would take from her what was hers. She sat up and arranged her cello between her knees, then looked at Phillip. He was staring at her with a look on his face she'd never seen directed at her before.

It was pity.

Something snapped inside of her. The calm, rational voice

she'd listened to for years was drowned out by a mad keening. This wasn't what she'd signed on for. Chelsea was proud and strong, and she'd be damned if a man would look at her with pity rather than burning desire. She knew something had happened. Something was changing. She didn't like it one bit.

He stared at her, his expression changing from pity to concern. His perfect brows furrowed above his sharp aquiline nose. She smiled at him as if nothing at all was wrong. He smiled back, nervously. Something was bothering him. His gaze darted to the side, then back down to his sheet music. She turned and looked to where he had glanced, and she saw that redheaded trumpet player Melody ogling him, giddy, naïve, and happy.

Chelsea felt a stab of rage. Happy? She'd fix that.

The practice session seemed to drag on interminably. Chelsea knew her playing was off, and her distraction was cheapening her performance, but she couldn't muster up the focus to care. Francis frowned at her, but technically she was playing perfectly. It was the *jeu ne sai quois* that was missing, that special something that made her one of the most esteemed cello players in the whole of the South, if not the country. They called her Cello Belle, but she was anything but a blushing country belle. Today, her notes were merely adequate, and she knew Francis would chalk it up to an off day. If it happened again, he'd speak with her. Until then, he let her play blandly through the day without comment.

She worked very hard not to look at Phillip or Melody.

Immediately after practice, Chelsea rushed to pack her instrument. She didn't want to speak with Phillip, or worse, allow him the closure of breaking off their non-romance. *He's not yours.* Distracted, it took her longer to collect her belongings than she'd intended. She heard someone approach. She'd know that gait anywhere, and her eyes caressed every angle of him on the way up to his face. There was that pitying look again. Molten fire roiled in her stomach.

"Chelsea, can we talk?" he said. He tipped his head toward a practice room. "Privately?"

She looked around the room. Melody was watching them, looking confused. Chelsea felt a surge of satisfaction so smug it momentarily eclipsed her anger.

"She doesn't know," she said, a note of sadistic glee sharpening her words.

Phillip frowned. He looked older when he frowned and less boyishly charming. She wanted him to be the bold, young man who'd taken her into a practice room to ravage her, not this new one who looked softer, less inclined to pin her to the piano bench as they tested the limits of the room's sound-proofing. Her stomach turned.

"Fine," she said sullenly.

They went to the room, and he shut the door. The click of the handle sounded the finality of a death sentence. Boy, she was morose today, and it was all Phillip's fault.

She rounded on him the second the door closed. "What the hell, Phillip? You're already moving on to the next young thing?"

"This has nothing to do with anyone else. It's been over for a while now. You know I haven't felt good about it for weeks," he said.

"Oh, I was just joking," she said, her voice a purr. "Are you *sure* you haven't felt good about it?"

She took a bold step forward to close the space between them. Her hand went to the buttons on his shirt and began to unfasten them. He took her hand in his and moved it away.

Chelsea was furious but undeterred. "I know what you feel good about." She stepped back, untucked her form-fitting black cotton shirt, then lifted it over her head and off, showing her perfect breasts cradled in a lacy red bra. She stepped close to him, pushed her body against his, and tilted her face upwards, angling for a kiss.

He put his hands on her shoulders and gently, but firmly, eased her away.

"Chelsea. I said it's over," he said. "This has nothing to do with anyone but you and me."

For all of her life, Chelsea had never understood the expression *seeing red*. She thought that it was some fantasy expression, a metaphor, but as she stood in front of Phillip, with the cold chill of the air conditioning hitting her bare stomach, the edges of her vision swam with crimson. His rejection stung every nerve of her body. She crossed her arms in front of her, gooseflesh prickling her shoulders. She was raging inside. How dare he use her and discard her? How dare he make her feel small? How dare he toss her aside for a childlike redhead, or worse, nobody at all?

A slap echoed in the room, and she was almost as shocked as Phillip that her hand had connected with his face. She grabbed her shirt from the piano bench and violently pulled it back on.

Phillip rubbed his cheek, staring at Chelsea with a mix of pity and anger. "I'm sorry it's ending this way."

"What way, with you not getting your dick wet?" she sneered. He looked disappointed. She wasn't usually so vulgar, and it was the second disturbingly out-of-character thing she'd done in the past five minutes.

"No, ending with you feeling so hurt," he said.

She stepped toward the door and, with her hand on the handle, tossed her hair over her shoulder. His guilelessness chafed her. She glared at him, full of hate.

"It's too late for you to pretend to care about my feelings," she said, slamming the door open and storming out.

Phillip watched her go, a pit forming in his stomach. He'd heard Chelsea talk about her former lovers with mild disdain, but he'd never seen this side of her. He hoped she'd be able to be professional, to move past it. They'd been friends for years, occasionally casual lovers, but their attraction had played out for longer over the last year when they'd both been single and wanted some physical company. Their chemistry was undeniable, but there was no real emotion behind it.

Or so Phillip had thought.

He sat at the piano and lifted the key cover. His fingers flew over some basic scales, already limber from a day of playing his violin. He transitioned into a Beethoven piece, then a Bartok, then an angry modern piece that suited his mood. He didn't hit all the notes right, and he had no sheet music, but he played from memory. If there was one thing he excelled at, it was using his memory.

His face dropped into a scowl. He remembered his first night with Chelsea, all cocktails and playful, sloppy kisses until, suddenly, he was on top of her. She was fumbling with his belt. He was hiking up her skirt. He was in her. She was screaming in pleasure, and then, they were both satisfied and soon asleep.

They'd talked over coffee the next day and agreed it was fun, but neither was looking to get into anything serious. They had kept it as it was, just friends, with raucous sex every so often. It was fine, fine for years, but over the last month, something had changed in Chelsea. She was more serious, more focused when they were together. There was a dark shadow over their trysts. He'd thought she was getting ready to end it, but every time he brought up ending things, she'd said *no*. Damn his soul, he'd been too weak to tell her no, once and for all.

The piano crescendoed, and his playing stopped abruptly, mid-phrase. Phillip could remember no more notes of that piece. The silence echoed and rang in his ears. He stood and closed the keyguard. The familiar and satisfying clunk made him feel better, at home. He stared at the piano for a moment, interrupted by a knock on the practice room door.

He opened it. Melody stood there, smiling at him. His heart expanded, feeling like it would burst from his chest. How had he only known her intimately for a day? She was wringing her hands, just a bit.

"I didn't want to bother you, but I was wondering if you wanted to get a bite to eat tonight?" she asked.

He grinned. "Are you asking me out on a date?"

Pink bloomed on her cheeks as she nodded, and Phillip wanted to gather her in his arms and kiss every freckle on her.

"Then I gratefully accept your invitation, mon cheri."

They walked out together, talking and laughing.

Across the parking lot, Chelsea sat silently in her car, watching them. She was not finished with Phillip. Not yet.

CHAPTER NINE

Rehearsal hadn't yet begun, and the room was a cacophony of warm-up scales and idle chatter. Francis clapped his hands to get the room's attention. The silence was immediate.

"As many of you know, we have been attempting to finalize the details for our first performance. This has been done."

A rumble of excitement ran through the room. This was, after all, what they had gathered to do. The thrill in the air was palpable.

"We will be performing in the Beaux Reve Bandshell at noon on the thirtieth of this month. I will be sending you the song list tonight."

He raised his arms, a baton held delicately aloft in his right hand. The room fell silent. A metal and wood rattle passed through the orchestra as everyone lifted their instruments. As Francis bounced his hands, the group played through their course of warm-up scales, then progressed to the pieces of music they'd be performing in two short weeks.

Melody could barely contain her excitement. As a member of this performance ensemble, she was paid a pittance for her rehearsal time, but performances were where she would make her rent money. Not a day too soon. She was out of savings and on the verge of taking her trumpet to the French Quarter to try her hand at busking. She could have wept with relief and joy. Paid to perform? That was her dream.

After the practice, she gathered her bags, trumpet, and sheet music. Melody had realized halfway through the day that she desperately needed to work on her solo, and timing was where she fell apart. She needed time with a metronome, and the ones in the practice rooms were far better to work with than the small, shrill digital one she had.

Phillip watched her enter the corner practice room. He drank in the view of her body. Her jeans hugged her perfectly curved hips as she strode to the door. He could remember the feel of her lips on his. He gathered up his own belongings and hurried into the practice room next to hers.

He played furiously, directing all his considerable sexual energy into the strings of his violin. The air conditioning pumped into the small room, but sweat ran down his face. He could hear the barest hint of Melody playing in the next room, and he stopped to listen. Placing where she was in the piece, he flipped through his own sheet music. He found the bar and put his violin under his chin. The notes poured from his instrument, every stanza an emotional plea through the walls. She dropped a note and recovered beautifully. He wondered if she heard him playing. He could feel her through the not-quite-perfect soundproofing. They played together, rising and falling, crescendoing, then letting the music ebb back into silence.

The piece had ended.

Phillip let the violin drop away from his chin. He stood, gently placing the instrument back into its case. No sooner had he settled it into the velvet than the door to his practice room burst open. Melody stood there, breathing heavily, her cheeks slightly flushed. She set her trumpet case down next to the doorframe. The door shut behind her, and before it clicked closed, she rushed toward him.

He gathered her into his arms, and their lips met. Hers parted, warm and metallic from her trumpet, and his tongue slid into her mouth. She wrapped her arms around him, and he grabbed a fistful of her curls in his hand. They staggered back. He pinned her against the wall, and she threw her legs around him. He ran his hand down her neck, over her shirt. Her nipples hardened, and he paused for a moment to run his fingers over them through her blouse. He was so focused on her, he felt every ridge of lace on her bra. She sighed, her breath hot on his face.

As if drawn in by a beacon, Phillip ran one hand down her stomach, unbuttoning her jeans with the other. He angled his fingers back, running his palm over the spreading dampness at the front of her underwear. She kissed him more passion-ately, and he snuck his fingers past the side of the thin cotton barrier and found the center of her wetness. He ran two fin-gers over it, beckoning her pleasure, then slid a finger into her. His thumb flicked her clit, and she moaned.

His lips left hers and moved to her ear. He nibbled at her lobe gently as she rode his hand. Her wetness ran down his fingers, and she tightened as she came closer to orgasm. He whispered into her ear. "What do you want me to do to you?" he growled.

"I want you in me," she gasped.

She clutched at his shoulders as he wrestled her jeans and underwear from her legs. Once she was freed, he slid his hands up the sides of her thighs and clutched her ass. She groped at the button of his slacks, and he grinned. He slid one hand farther around her, and his fingers found her slick wet-ness again. She gasped against his neck, unzipped his fly, and he sprang free. He brought his hand and her closer to the head of his throbbing cock. He slid his fingers from her, and she eased herself onto him. She rocked her hips, and he thrust into her. They both moaned in pleasure, finding their rhythm. She clutched him with her legs, riding his hips and bucking so hard, he almost lost his balance. The pressure grew as his pleasure grew until he gritted his teeth to hold back the flood of ecstasy. Just when he didn't think he could restrain himself any longer, her legs gripped him even more tightly, and she dug her fingers into his shoulders, muffling her scream into his neck.

He let loose his own wave of ecstasy, pumping into her. She rocked her hips as he twitched inside of her. The two stayed still for a moment, pulses racing, catching their breath. Phillip looked into Melody's eyes, almost shyly. He felt such a surge of warmth and joy he almost wanted to cry.

"How do you make me so happy?" she asked.

He grinned a half-cocked smile. "Sheer luck," he answered.

He gently set her down so her feet touched the floor, though her head was still in the clouds. She'd never felt that way about anyone. His raw physical appeal was only enhanced by his warmth and humor. She couldn't take her eyes off him. She drank in the view of him, and when he looked at her, she felt like the best version of herself she could be. She wanted to stay there with him, in this room, just staring at him, forever.

But alas, the real world outside that door called to them. It had been a long day of practice, and they had stayed even later. Melody's stomach rumbled, and they both laughed.

"Me too," he said, straightening himself out with a series of tucks and zips. "How about that dinner?"

She smiled, smoothed her shirt down, then patted her hair. He reached out and tucked a stray curl behind her ear. She blushed, and his hand stopped at her ear. He ran his thumb over her reddened cheek and leaned in to kiss her lips, gently. She rested her hand on his chest and felt his heartbeat through his skin, his shirt. Lips still pressed firmly to his, she sighed and leaned in closer.

His stomach rumbled, and they laughed again, giddy and in love.

They left the room holding each other's hands, their respective instrument cases in their other hand. Chelsea was sitting in her symphony chair, flipping through sheet music, her cello gripped between her legs. She barely looked up when they came out. Melody dropped Phillip's hand and tried to pretend they'd merely been practicing music. They had their instruments, after all.

"Good night, Chelsea!" said Melody. She couldn't hide the happiness in her voice or the springs in her steps.

The cellist didn't even look their way.

CHAPTER TEN

Chelsea's stomach was on fire. She couldn't believe what she'd just seen. The two of them, leaving the room she and Phillip had christened just a few days before. Hand in hand, bold as you please, and that little tart had the nerve to wish her a good night? A good night? After that?

How had she missed them going into that room together? The rooms might really have been more soundproof than she thought. She hadn't heard Melody moaning, although she was sure that Phillip could make her scream. Maybe they *had* been practicing music. She hadn't heard them playing, but soundproofing could have prevented that.

She felt like she was losing her mind. Chelsea reminded herself again that she and Phillip weren't an exclusive item. They had enjoyed each other's bodies when they had been single. She had no claim on him, on his brooding dark brown eyes, his cheerful smile, his solid stomach, and broad shoulders. Oh, god, when had she developed feelings for him? Maybe she was just jealous because she couldn't have him at her leisure anymore. Was that it? She didn't know.

Chelsea was never someone to be unsure of things. This new state of being was uncomfortable and made her angry in a way that made her consider dark things that might make her feel better. She wondered if she could find Melody's family's number, call them, and tell them what a snotty little bitch they'd raised. No, that wouldn't do. They probably already knew. If they didn't, they were ignorant fools, and she probably wouldn't be able to convince them.

Did Melody have any friends she could turn against her? Chelsea wracked her brain but could only ever remember Melody talking to that Back o' Town trumpeter who was probably loyal to a damn fault. Chelsea sighed. How in the world would she repay that little whore's treachery? She ran the bow across the strings of the cello and pondered it. Violence seemed so gauche. It wasn't truly beneath her, but it didn't seem like it would be satisfying enough. She'd probably be arrested, too. How then, to get back at the interloper without compromising her own position?

The notes flew from the cello as if they were independent of Chelsea. She paused. She'd been playing a dark, melancholy tune from Mussorgsky, a song about an ox, one about the sadness and toil of work yet to be done.

She knew, then, she would do whatever it took to bring Melody Bell down. Not necessarily to hurt her, physically, but to humiliate her, to break her spirit. She looked at the empty doorway where Phillip and Melody had just exited and drew her bow across her strings one more time. The cello yelped, almost as if it was laughing. *Oh, Melody, I will destroy you.*

Melody swirled a French fry in a bit of ketchup.

Phillip made a face. "I don't know how you can eat that stuff."

"What, ketchup?" She grinned and popped the fry into her mouth. "It's the best. Why, what do you put on your fries?"

He grinned and grabbed a bottle of hot sauce from a condiment caddy on the table. Melody watched with her mouth open as he let droplets fall onto his fries. He offered her the plate, and she took one gingerly. After a moment's hesitation, she took a nibble. His heart swelled as he watched the tip of her nose wiggle as she chewed, then wrinkled her face. Her cheeks turned pink, and he wanted to kiss her rosy blush. The warmth of new love spread through his stomach and lower.

"No! That's so spicy!" she squealed. She grabbed her beer and took a few quick gulps, sticking out her tongue afterward. "You know I'm from Ohio."

He reached across the table for her hand. He ran his thumb over her soft knuckles, amazed that such a mundane part of a woman's body could be so alluring. Her mouth was reddened from the heat of the sauce, and he could barely move his eyes from her lips.

"Phillip, this is crazy. We met just a few weeks ago, but I feel like I've known you my whole life," she said.

"I feel the same way," he said and gently squeezed her hand.

She took his hand in both of hers and lifted the back of it to her cheek. Every hair on the back of his hand strummed with pleasure as he touched her face. He gazed at her, wondering what he'd done to be so lucky for Melody Bell to allow him to love her. He wanted to drink her in with every pore, and when their gazes met, he was sure she felt the same. As he reveled in her touch, breathing in the smell of her, he believed nothing could ever go wrong when she was nearby.

CHAPTER ELEVEN

M elody settled into her chair and chatted with her neighboring musicians.

"The Saints are gonna go all the way this year. You mark me, hear?" said Bette, a broad-shouldered, good-natured euphonium player said from behind her.

"Ha! Never gonna happen," laughed Martin, a trumpet player two chairs down.

"Aww, you guys, they don't have a chance against the Browns!" said Melody.

The group was silent for a moment, and Melody tried to keep a straight face as they all looked at each other, trying to decide if she was joking or if she hadn't been following her team's miserable season. She couldn't resist the smile she was fighting anymore. As soon as she grinned, both rows erupted in laughter. It was the easy camaraderie of people who liked to work and laugh together, even if the jokes weren't nearly as funny as the people telling them.

Chelsea spun in her chair and glared at the brass sections. Half of them saw it and quieted immediately. Melody was in too good of a mood to let the sour cellist ruin her fun. She leaned forward. Chelsea's back was already turned toward her.

"Hey, Chelsea, do you watch football?"

Chelsea's shoulders rose slightly, and she turned slowly. With every millimeter she turned, Melody's blood cooled. By the time Chelsea had turned enough to face her, Melody had gooseflesh on her arms. Her stomach dropped. Chelsea's glare was so icy the whole brass section busied themselves doing absolutely anything to keep from looking at her, from rustling through sheet music, emptying spit valves, to applying oil to their instruments.

"It doesn't matter if I watch football or not, does it? I'm not going to chat with you about football, or the weather, or our feelings, or anything. I'm not here to make friends. I'm not here to hear about your thoughts on the Saints. I'm not here to hear your vacuous thoughts, period. I'm here to play music. If you insist on dragging the brass section down a professional level or two with your chatter, feel free, but don't think for a second that strings will follow your shoddy lead."

Chelsea spun around in her chair, her stony face disappearing as her glossy hair whipped after her. Melody was completely taken aback. She leaned against her chair, stunned. Did her cheerful chattiness really come across as unprofessionalism? Tears sprang to her eyes. No, she would not cry. *That* was most definitely not professional. She took a deep breath and squared her shoulders.

"Music *is* feelings, Chelsea. I'm not asking you to be anyone's best friend, but we do have to know and trust each other to play well together," said a deep male voice.

Francis was standing at the door with Anna, the two of them watching the room with the heavy gaze of a larger perspective. Francis was looking at Chelsea, but Melody noticed how Anna was looking angrily elsewhere in the room. She followed Anna's gaze and saw, with surprise, that she was glaring at Phillip. Why would she be angry with Phillip? How could anyone be angry with Phillip?

Chelsea didn't move a single muscle. She was furious at Francis, but it wouldn't do for her to verbally parry with him in front of the group. For that matter, ever. Francis was not a patient man when he was challenged, and he suffered no fools. He was fair-minded and honest almost to a fault, but Chelsea knew she was not being fair, rational, or even remotely kind. He would not hesitate to tell her exactly how childish she was being, and in the world of symphonies, she could not afford to gain a reputation for acting like a scorned lover if a relationship went sideways.

Musicians could be a temperamental lot, but professional musicians were almost always able to set aside that impetuousness and channel their passions into music. To be honest, it was impossible to get to a professional performance level without the ability to practice for hours on end, to set aside your emotions, and keep focusing on the incremental improvements that come from days and years of frustration and failure.

This wasn't *her* failure. Chelsea had done everything right. She was emotionally undemanding, a fantastic lover, beautiful, witty, and charming. He still didn't love her. He loved, instead, this interloper from Ohio. She saw it clearly written across his face. The little tart who thought she might be able to befriend Chelsea with football chit chat. The girl who had goaded her into receiving stern words from Francis. Molten anger seethed in Chelsea's stomach. How dare she? How *dare* she come into Chelsea's city, steal away Chelsea's man, steal the affections of Chelsea's orchestra? She, *Chelsea*, was supposed to be the darling of the group. *She* was supposed to be the leader everyone turned to when they had questions about the emotions of a piece, but instead, they were turning to this redheaded moppet, this *Ohioan*. This *outsider*. Chelsea seethed.

Something must be done.

Phillip, on the other side of the room, was studiously avoiding Anna's gaze. He recalled a conversation they'd had the other day and now felt thoroughly ashamed. She had known something was happening and pulled him into Francis's office when the conductor was out.

With no preamble, Anna had asked him, "Are you sleeping with Melody?" She was never one to mince words.

The blood had drained from his face, leaving his cheeks feeling deflated and cool. "How did you . . ."

"I know everything about this group, Phillip. It's my job," she replied, her voice strained, each syllable clipped.

"We didn't mean for . . ."

She'd held up her hand. Her fingers were long, graceful, and bedecked with huge sparkling rings. Her face was inscrutable. He had no idea what she might be thinking, only that it certainly didn't including feeling more respect for Phillip than she'd had before.

"You need to make it right with Chelsea before this goes any farther," she said.

His jaw dropped open. "How . . ."

"Phillip, I just told you. It's my job to know *everything* about this symphony. That means the dynamics of the entire group, including who may be having carnal relations with whom. You, sir, have been stringing Chelsea along for quite some time, I believe."

"Stringing? We talked about it and . . ."

Anna killed his next words with a look. Her perfectly penciled brow arched, and the words stuck in his throat. "You may have *talked about it,* but that did not stop her from falling in a bit of love with you, even if it is a sick and crippled kind of love that can't grow because it is not reciprocated? It is up to you to assuage her now, to make her feel as if she is a whole person again. Not a cast-off."

Phillip's cheeks burned, then and now. His emotions ran deep, and his shame over his affair with Chelsea was almost unbearable. Chelsea wasn't disposable, but he had treated her badly. Still, he'd tried to end it multiple times, and she'd said no. Another voice inside his head said he hadn't exactly fought off her advances with vigor. He sighed heavily, acutely aware of the mixed messages he'd been sending. *We're over unless you pursue me harder. We're over unless you really want this to continue. We're over, unless . . . unless I find someone else.* That was the sad truth of it. He felt awful. Chelsea was better than that. She deserved better, and he knew it.

He turned to look at Chelsea. A chill ran over his spine. She did not look like anyone who should be pitied. Her perfect pale skin stood out against her dark hair, and her sharp features were even more chiseled by anger. *She knows. How can she know?*

Of course, they'd been sloppy. Leaving rehearsal hand-in-hand, getting lost looking at each other while the world fell away. Of course, the world didn't fall away. People were still there, with their eyes to see. Chelsea was still there.

Phillip looked at Melody, who had shrunk into her chair like a chastised child. He could tell her feelings were hurt, and for good reason. She'd extended an emotional hand to Chelsea, and Chelsea had swatted it away with a verbal ax, while Melody had no idea why. Phillip felt sick. He'd done this. He'd dragged Melody into a quagmire. Chelsea could be funny and charming, but she was also fierce and could be prickly. He hadn't considered that Melody might be exposed to Chelsea's anger, because he hadn't considered the possibility of Chelsea caring about their relationship ending.

Their relationship. Oh, dear. He had to admit that was what it was, even though they'd agreed to keep it casual. He had feelings for Chelsea. They'd known each other for ages, but his were the relaxed feelings of friends. Of a person you took for granted who were just there, through so much of your life, and you thought you knew them inside and out. It was impossible to know someone if you assumed things about them, and he'd assumed. It had never occurred to him that she would develop something more for him.

He glanced from Melody to Chelsea. What was he going to do to make this better? Was there anything he could do?

Melody had seen Anna's glare at Phillip but had barely registered it before she retreated into her own complicated feelings. She was too distracted by Chelsea's outburst. Why did the cellist hate her so much? She had heard stories of Southerners being resistant to Northern folks, but this was truly next level animosity. So much for Southern Hospitality.

Now, Chelsea had been chastised. As much as Melody felt a little surge of gratitude for Francis's words, she also knew, from Chelsea's recent outburst, just how awful it felt to be called out in front of a room of people. She felt a surge of sympathy for Chelsea. Even though the woman had been short with her, she did feel an inexplicable kinship with her and wanted to make things right.

She'd set things right. She had to.

The rest of the morning's rehearsal was uneventful. They played through the pieces, notes were hit impeccably, and Francis deemed the rehearsal successful. It seemed the entire room had forgotten about the incident between Melody and Chelsea, except for Melody and probably Chelsea.

"The time is now 12:05, musicians. Please be back and ready to play at 1:35. We will begin with the Mueller. Enjoy your lunch," said Francis.

As Chelsea gently settled her cello into its velvet casing, Melody approached her.

"Chelsea," she said. The dark-haired woman looked up at her with surprise, then anger. "I'm sorry if I offended you this morning. I . . . I was wondering if I could buy you a coffee?"

Chelsea's face was unreadable. There was a long, uncomfortable pause. "I will accept your coffee, Melody, but it does not mean that we will be friends by the time it is drunk."

Melody nodded.

"I can deal with that," she said. "You pick the place."

CHAPTER TWELVE

The cafe Chelsea chose was two short blocks away, but the walk felt like it took months. They were silent the entire time. The two women settled into a pair of identical wrought iron chairs. A tiny mosaic-topped table seemed barely substantial enough to hold two drinks aloft, much less to put the kind of distance between the women that Chelsea wanted. The strains of brass music floated faintly on the breeze, and the heavy muddy river smell of the Mississippi lingered over them. Melody had a sandwich and an iced tea in front of her. Chelsea clutched a cup of coffee and stared down a plate of fruit. Chelsea sipped the hot coffee and raised her eyes to look at Melody, who was visibly uncomfortable.

Chelsea had made up her mind to be unflappable.

Melody picked at the wrapper of her sandwich. "I want to apologize for this morning," she started.

Chelsea stared at her icily, popping a grape into her mouth. She let her gaze drop to Melody's sandwich, then back to her freckled face. Her ocular judgment had its intended effect, and Melody's face reddened.

"Oh?" said Chelsea.

"Yes, I didn't realize that we were distracting you, and I just wanted to include you . . ." Melody trailed off lamely.

Chelsea dabbed at the corners of her mouth with a napkin and leaned forward, her gaze, hypnotizing and dangerous like a cobra's, she hoped, locked on Melody's. "Include me in what exactly? Your chit-chat club?"

"I . . . well . . . the group?" stammered Melody.

Chelsea smiled then, a wry half-smile that wilted Melody's resolve.

"Honey, I don't need to be included in any club of which you are a member."

Only I do. The loved by Phillip club. She tried to shove the thought from her mind. That club should only have one member, and it *should* be her. She seethed but reminded herself of her resolve to be icy cool.

"Why do you hate me so much?" asked Melody. She had stopped picking at her sandwich and looked at Chelsea steadily.

Oh, no! Was this the famous Midwestern directness? Well, the only thing to do about that was to break out the big guns with Southern Debutante Dismissiveness. With a jolt of glee, she realized that Melody still had absolutely no idea that Chelsea and Phillip had a past.

"Oh, Melody honey," she said, as sarcastically as she could, "I don't hate you."

She reached over and patted her on the arm. She was delighted to see Melody's arm prickle with gooseflesh.

"I don't think about you at all," she said and stood. She picked up her coffee and turned away. Over her shoulder, she said, "Thanks for the coffee."

Chelsea strode toward their brick building, sipping the coffee Melody had bought for her. Even though it was from her favorite cafe, it tasted bitter and foul today. She blamed Melody. Chelsea was calm on the outside, but inside, she was busy stuffing her anger into a little place deep inside of her soul.

Her mind worked over their conversation, tucking information into boxes for later use.

Melody was afraid of her.

She didn't have any idea about Phillip's past with Chelsea.

She was absolutely dying to belong to a group.

As she tossed her still-scalding coffee into a trash bin with more violence than was necessary, her mouth twisted into a malevolent smile. She could work with that.

CHAPTER THIRTEEN

Phillip had seen Melody approach Chelsea and the two of them leave together, and he saw Chelsea arriving now, solo. It gave him an uneasy feeling. He sat on the bench across from the building and ate his lunch. He chewed his turkey sandwich slowly and thought about that morning.

He had thought Chelsea would understand when it finally ended. There had been no reason to stop before, other than Phillip's reservations. Chelsea had brushed his feelings aside, and he thought he might be ridiculous for ending a good thing — or at the least, an okay thing. They did have good sex, but his heart wasn't in it. The last few months before the symphony had started wore on his conscience. He'd known it was over, but he hadn't possessed the strength to resist Chelsea's beauty. They'd had some good times, though now he realized that was what made it harder on Chelsea now.

As she approached, he set aside his sandwich and stood. She motioned for him to sit. He did, then picked up his things to clear room for her next to him. Chelsea sat, delicately, on the edge of the bench.

"What was that all about this morning?" he asked. "You snapping at the trumpets."

"It was so absurd. Melody tried to engage me in a conversation about football. Can you imagine?" She laughed, abrupt and harsh-sounding.

"I don't know why that's so funny," he said.

She scowled. "Look, Phillip, I know you're smitten with her *talent*, but you can't expect the rest of us to be so taken."

His face warmed, and he felt a pulse in his forehead.

Chelsea sat up straighter. "I mean, she plays wonderfully, and I'm sure she is a *lovely* person." The words came out flat as her jaw clenched. "I don't know her, and you know how I loathe football."

Phillip stared at Chelsea. How much did she know about him and Melody? Or perhaps she was just jealous of the attention Melody received from everyone for her musical talent and natural charisma. In any case, it was time for honesty.

"Chelsea, I have to tell you something," Phillip said.

Chelsea moved her hand to her stomach. It rested there for a moment, still and pale, until she slid it ever so slightly lower.

"Oh, good, I have something I need to tell you too," she said, rubbing her hand gently over her abdomen. Phillip's eyes went wide, and he paled. "You go first," she purred.

"Why . . . why don't you go ahead?" he stammered.

She batted her eyes downward, looking at her hand. Phillip froze, staring at her abdomen.

"Well, there is one rather specific reason I've been so emotional lately," she said.

Phillip sat silent, shocked. His face was stone. "No," he said. "That doesn't make any . . ."

"Oh, Phillip," she said, her eyes shining with tears. "Of course it does. How many times did we fool around, not bothering with any protection?"

"You said you were on the pill," he said, his voice low. His mind raced. The timing of this revelation felt suspicious.

"I am, but it's not one hundred percent effective, and, well, I guess we were in that small percentage. We are going to be parents, Phillip."

He stared at her blankly. This felt wrong, impossible. She had to be lying. She just had to be. One of her crocodile tears ran down her perfect, pale cheek. She reached her hand toward his cheek.

"You're going to be a wonderful father," she said.

He swatted her hand away. She blinked in shock. He felt sick as he remembered a long-ago conversation they'd had. "You told me once that you pulled this on Henri," he said.

She stared at him for a moment. "Exactly, why would I lie to you now?"

"If I find out you're lying . . ."

She jumped to her feet. "How could you! Why would I lie about this?"

"Because you don't want us to be over," he said flatly. He stood slowly, methodically, and loomed over her. She looked small from this angle, frail but dangerous, like a scorpion. "You cannot hear me when I say to you that it's done, that it's been done for so long, and some of that is my fault for leading you on."

"How could you? We are going to have a baby, Phillip, so you need to get your shit together and be an adult."

He shook his head. "I'll go with you to the doctor to get a pregnancy test, but until then, I do not believe you."

"I can't believe that after everything we've been through," she sobbed out, "you'd doubt me about this."

She slumped on the bench and cried into her hands. He sat down next to her and put a hand on her back. Her heaving sobs didn't match her breathing, and he wondered if this suspicious anxiety was what Henri had felt all those years ago.

CHAPTER FOURTEEN

Phillip stood, slid his hand into his pocket, and pulled out a handkerchief, then handed it to Chelsea.

Chelsea delicately dabbed her eyes and nose with it, then dried her tears, taking care not to smudge her makeup. If that left her eyes a bit redder than they had been, so be it, but she knew her flawless face was undisturbed. She handed the handkerchief back to him.

He held up his hand. "No, Chels, you keep it. If you are lying to me, it'll be something to remember me by."

Phillip turned on his heel and stormed back to the building.

Chelsea reached over and picked up his abandoned sandwich. She took a bite and smiled. The seed was planted.

She spotted a mass of curly hair bobbing down the street toward her, catching the light with its offensive copper glow. A warm sense of satisfaction grew in her chest. She smiled more widely and took another bite of Phillip's sandwich.

Melody kept her focus on the ground as she walked toward the main doors. Her hands were in her pockets, and she looked sad, boyish, and pathetic.

Chelsea wanted to kick her in the shins.

She reminded herself that she was winning, and she felt almost sorry for the girl. She had no idea who she was up against. If Phillip hadn't told Melody about their previous dalliance—which she was certain he hadn't, the poor hopeless romantic that he was—then Melody didn't even know she was up against anything at all.

Chelsea stopped mid-chew. Had she just considered

herself Phillip's former lover? Oh, that wouldn't do at all. She glared at Melody, who slunk into the building without even a hint of her usual cheer and energy. *You've ruined everything. Now I'll ruin you.*

She reached a hand idly to her chest, realizing with a start that she was reaching for the gris-gris bag that had been there the past week. It had stayed around her neck for seven days, then she'd tucked it under her mattress, just like the shop-keeper had said.

The afternoon passed uneventfully, more fine-tuning of the pieces, the orchestra preparing for their performance that was drawing closer by the day. Melody tried to focus on the music, but her mind kept going back to Chelsea dismissing her so completely. There was some reason for it. She knew there was. Maybe Melody reminded her of someone Chelsea didn't like. She kept turning it over in her head, determined to get to the bottom of it. Surely there was some way to smooth over whatever conflict had sprung up between them.

After practice, Melody packed her things away and watched the beautiful cellist prepare to leave for the evening. Because rehearsals were running longer as the performance approached, many of them had taken to leaving their instruments in the practice room. Francis securely locked the room after they'd all left for the evening, and Anna came so early in the morning to run the office that there were only a few hours their precious instruments were left alone, and even for those few hours, they were safe behind two separate sets of locked doors. After rehearsing for twelve to fourteen hours, few people were keen on practicing at home. Those who were so inclined came in with bags under their eyes. Because the limited time outside of the hall could be spent practicing or sleeping, their performances suffered, and they eventually left their instruments there too.

Phillip approached Melody, and though she was distracted by the events of the day, she noticed he seemed to be acting strangely.

"Is everything okay?" she asked.

"What, no hello?" he said, though he seemed preoccupied.

The joy she had felt with him just a few short hours ago was dulled by her altercation with Chelsea and now his sudden distance.

"You wanna get dinner?" he asked.

She nodded, and as if on cue, her stomach growled. Tension broken, they laughed and walked out the door.

The day's events weighed on her mind over dinner. They ate in silence.

Phillip, in particular, sat utterly lost in thought. He came back to the moment with a jolt, looking at Melody in front of him as if seeing her for the first time that day. "Sorry, what was that?" he asked.

"Oh, I didn't say anything." She frowned. "What's going on? I mean, I know I'm not the greatest company right now, but . . ."

"You're amazing company. I could just stare at you all day long, not saying a word, and have a ball."

Melody blushed. A warmth spread through her stomach that was more than the delicious gumbo she was eating. She reached her hand toward Phillip's. His hand met hers halfway, and their fingers threaded together. His touch electrified her skin. She felt everything, the warmth of his touch, the weight of the shirt on her shoulder, her nipples rubbing the lace of her bra. She heard the thudding beat of her heart and reveled in the cool air caressing her lips as she breathed in.

Phillip had been lost in thought about the bombshell Chelsea had dropped on him that afternoon. He didn't believe her, though the fallout, if she was telling the truth, would be awful. Not, however, the reality of becoming a father. He'd always wanted children, but he was torn. Chelsea had told him something, and he hadn't believed her. He wanted to be a good man. He wanted that desperately, but he knew everything about his tryst with Chelsea was not good. He wasn't a casual person, not some playboy who could just have cheap sex with no emotion. It made him feel terrible, and he felt even worse because he had known Chelsea was not entirely free of emotion herself. He'd kept at it anyway, letting those feelings grow, even as his conscience gnawed at him and begged him to stop. His body had betrayed him with its desire for her smooth flesh.

Should he believe his body when it reacted to Melody? Because react it did. They were holding hands across a cafe table, and his body was responding as if they were lying side-by-side, naked, kissing deeply, and caressing every inch of each other. He was throbbing, aching for her. He needed her, and he could see the color rising in Melody's face.

"Should we get this to go?" he asked.

She nodded, her gaze locked on his.

They careened back to her place, his driving faster and less controlled than usual. They held hands, and he gently fondled the tips of her fingers with his. He could see her squirming in the seat, looking at him and then back at the road as if she was willing him to arrive at the house already.

He squealed into a parking spot just outside of her door, and they had barely stepped out of the car doors before she launched herself into his arms. He lifted her feet from the ground to kiss her fully. His erection was pushing against his zipper so hard he thought it would rip the fabric of his pants if he bent to kiss her.

Every molecule of Melody's body vibrated. The firm head of his erection pushed against her hip, and she was glad he had picked her up. She wasn't sure her legs could support her. She wrapped them around him, and he carried her to the door. Their tongues danced together, in and out of their mouths, increasing their shared passion.

Melody fumbled for her keys, then tried clumsily to unlock the door. She shook and Phillip breathed heavily as he set her on her feet. She giggled as she struggled to unlock the door, and Phillip laughed. He rested his hands on her shoulders as she clicked the lock open and yanked the keys from the door. The warmth rising from her was intoxicating in the damp New Orleans air. He wrapped his arms around her stomach and drew her against him. His firm chest, his strong arms, and the long, hard length of him pressed against her.

She spun around, peeling her shirt from her body.

Phillip stepped back and watched. He pulled at his shirt and untucked the bottom, undoing the buttons as he watched Melody.

She stared at him, drinking in the sight of the olive skin covering his taut chest, the dark hair inviting her fingers to run through it. Instead, she undid the button of her jeans, sliding them off just as Phillip shrugged off his shirt. She stood in her lacy thong and bra, her skin begging for his touch. Melody eyed the conspicuous bulge under the soft cotton of his boxer briefs. Her knees felt weak.

She turned and beckoned him toward the bedroom. He closed the distance between them and wrapped his arms around her. She melted against his rippling muscles. He gathered her small frame into his arms and swept her to the bed. It creaked as Phillip settled her onto it. She sat at the edge, filled with unbridled lust. Phillip leaned down and kissed her, his lips gentle and firm. He parted his lips, and she followed his lead. She leaned back and spread her legs, and he followed her onto the bed.

She ran her hands over his shoulders as they kissed and ran her leg up his. Her lace and his cotton formed the barest barrier between them. He slid his hand up her back and deftly unhooked her bra with a single hand. She smiled against his lips as her bra fell away and her breasts were free. His palm slid up her side, over her breast, and paused at her nipple. He tweaked it gently with his thumb and forefinger, kissing her even as she gasped at the stimulation. He moved his lips down the side of her face to her neck and then, lower, to her breasts. Sweat beaded on her skin, and he kissed it away.

She ran her hands through his hair as he worked on her nipple with his lips, then, gently, his teeth. When she thought she might go mad with lust, he moved to her other breast. His hardness pressed against her, and she slid her hands from his hair to his shoulders, then back, to his hips. She slid her fingers under the waistband of his underwear and eased them down. They caught on his erection, the length of him catching on the elastic. They both giggled then, and he paused to help her strip them off. He took the opportunity to kiss her stomach, working his way ever lower to the very edge of her black lace panties. He kissed her through the lace, and her pulse raced against his lips.

He slid his hands up to the lace covering her hips and worked it down, slowly. Melody bit her lip as he followed the pace of the lace with his tongue. The fabric held her legs too close together for him to work his tongue into her innermost folds, and she quivered. She lifted her hips to him, and he pulled the panties past her ankles, off entirely. He ran his hand up the inside of her leg, caressing her soft inner thigh with his rough, calloused hand. He kissed the length of her leg, her breath quickening as he approached the junction of her thighs. She parted her legs for him, and he gently spread her open like the petals of a flower, kissing the inside of her lips, licking and teasing her clit with his tongue.

As he explored her with his tongue, he slowly slid one finger into her, then two. She gasped and rocked her hips as he gently moved his fingers with her. He found the firmer part of her inside and stroked it with his two digits. He stroked and licked, and she moaned so loudly the neighbor's dog began to bark. The moment the sensations overwhelmed her, she arched off the bed. Phillip followed her with his mouth, her toes curled, and a hot spurt of liquid poured from her.

Melody breathed heavily as she shook with the aftereffects of her wild orgasm, but she parted her legs wide as Phillip brought himself up to hover over her. She wrapped her legs around him and drew him into her, his back arching. He was so hard Melody thought she might split open, but she took the length of him easily. She rocked her hips. His eyes met hers. They were shining with ecstasy.

"Oh, god, Phillip! Oh god!" she moaned.

Every muscle of Melody's body tightened, and she arched wildly.

"Oh god! Oh god!" she shrieked.

Phillip's hips picked up a furious rhythm, and he thrust as he erupted, three times, deeply, with a feral growl. He collapsed onto her, sweating and spent. Melody was splayed out beneath him, panting. He rolled off her, onto his side, and gathered her into his arms. They shivered together, though the room was warm and humid.

"That was amazing," she said.

"*You* were amazing," he said.

They kissed tenderly, and she thought she would never be happier.

Later, as Phillip stroked Melody's hair and she drifted off to sleep, he turned the conversation he'd had with Chelsea over and over in his head. She couldn't possibly be. Could she? The timing seemed suspicious, but he'd known plenty of people who'd had accidents. He stared at Melody and wondered how in the world he would tell her. She snored lightly, but he couldn't sleep.

CHAPTER FIFTEEN

Melody and Phillip arrived together the next morning. Anna beckoned Phillip into her office. Melody waved at him in an attempt at being casual and chummy in a nothin'-to-see-here-but-some-colleagues attitude. She hoped nobody noticed the smoldering heat emanating from her body towards his or the look of raw desire she saw in his eyes.

She worked the valves of her trumpet, trying not to imagine that the plunging of the valve was so similar to the very activity that had kept her up so late last night. Heat crept to her cheeks, and she blew a few notes to muffle her smile and giggle. She knew this giddiness was only a temporary phase of a relationship, but she intended to ride the wave as long as she could.

Renny leaned over to her. "Be careful, mon cher. I hear Chelsea has it in for you," he whispered.

A fist of anxiety slammed into Melody's gut. "I think she doesn't really care about me," she mumbled, unsure.

At that moment, Chelsea slowly turned in her seat and looked directly at Melody. She smiled. All the heat and joy she'd created with Phillip drained from her body. Chelsea's smile had no warmth, no friendliness. It was the smile of a cat about to bite the head from a bird or the wide too-many-toothed grin of a shark. Then, she winked.

Tears spring to Melody's eyes as Chelsea swiveled around to the front of the room.

"Oh, she care, cher. She definitely care," said Renny. "You in trouble, girl."

Melody took a deep, shaky breath. What could Chelsea do to her? They were colleagues, after all, and they had to focus on their upcoming performance. It was their first public show. The first time they'd justify all of the money their financiers had given them. If they put on a good show, people might take notice, start to come to shows, pay to come. That was how you built yourself a name. Chelsea wouldn't possibly endanger that for, what, a comment about football?

There had to be some other reason she hated Melody so much. Melody, never one to back down, was determined to find out.

The days of rehearsal came and went. Francis declared they were as ready as they were going to be, and they should all feel good about tomorrow's performance. They would meet here, at the practice hall, warm up, then they would walk across the park to the bandshell. It was perfect. They were close enough to walk, and there was a smooth, paved path for the percussionists to roll their equipment. The weather was forecast to be lovely, warm and sunny, without a drop of rain.

The day of the show, Phillip awoke cradling Melody in his arms. She smiled against his shoulder. Her hair was wild from the night before, and as she moved, it brushed Phillip's chin. He sighed and rolled onto his back. Melody turned her face to his, and his bleary gaze met hers.

"G'morning," he said.

"Good morning," she replied and kissed his lips. "Happy performance day."

He grinned a grin of boyish glee. This was what he, Anna, and Francis had imagined for so long. It was beyond his wildest dreams that he'd fallen in love along the way.

She kicked the covers off and rose, nude. The morning light

illuminated her pale skin, and Phillip's heart swelled. He heard some far-off music playing, but he wasn't sure if it was coming from somewhere in the city or from deep in his mind. He sat up, swung his legs off the bed. She peeked coyly over her shoulder.

"Like what you see, Mr. Concertmaster?"

He chuckled. "I love what I see," he replied. He had intended it to be lighthearted, but the emotion weighed heavy in the words.

She turned to face him. "What?"

"I said, I love what I see," he repeated, more serious now. "I love you, Melody."

Melody knelt next to the bed. Phillip took her chin in his hand and tilted her face toward his. He looked deeply into her eyes and felt as if he were drowning in the bright green of her irises. He could stay there, staring into her eyes, forever.

She stared back, the warmth of his brown eyes enveloping her soul like an ethereal hug. She put her hands on his knees and leaned toward him. They kissed, gently, perfectly. She rose and sat next to him on the bed. Her bare skin pressed against his, but there was no desperate lust, only a calm satisfaction. He put his arm over her shoulders and breathed in the smell of her, sweet and feral and, inexplicably, like home. She leaned into him. He ran his fingers through her hair, and her eyes closed in pleasure.

"I love you too, Phillip," she said.

They reclined onto the bed and kissed, slowly. He felt her lips with every nerve in his. When he entered her, it was gentle. When they climaxed, together, they gasped and shuddered and held each other even closer.

Afterward, they lay next to each other, peaceful and calm, occasionally looking over at the other and smiling. Phillip turned onto his side to look at Melody, his head resting on a crooked arm. "I suppose we should start getting ready and head over," he said.

Melody ran her hand over his chest, sighed, and nodded. "It's showtime," she said, smiling.

Showers, coffee, and primping came and went. They walked out the door and into Phillip's car together, excited for the day. By the time they arrived at the practice hall, they'd laughed about a dozen different topics. They were still laughing as they entered the room, but their mirth shriveled and died in their throats when they saw the icy stare from Chelsea. Phillip experienced a wave of anger and fury so deep and violent he thought he might be having a seizure.

He wasn't.

The wave receded, and Phillip was left with a chilly confusion. It was the reaction of a man whose heart knew the truth, no matter what someone was telling him, and whose love was deeper for Melody than his anger was for Chelsea. He decided then and there if Chelsea was telling the truth, he would support her financially, and he would be a father to that child, but he would continue to grow the singular and miraculous love he felt with Melody.

If she still wants to be with you, after finding out? He couldn't quash the tiny voice of anxiety.

The two of them took their seats and began to warm up. Melody played a few scales. The look from Chelsea had sent shudders up her spine, and her skin still crawled. Her nerves were beginning to act up, and she thought she smelled something strange and astringent. She sniffed the air around her, but it was just a faint scent at the edge of her awareness. It reminded her of grade school, but she couldn't place it. Her first valve seemed a little sluggish, so she added a drop of oil to it and worked it in. It seemed to help, and the rest of her warmup went smoothly. She thought she caught Chelsea glancing at her occasionally, or was it her imagination? She thought she saw a smug smile on Chelsea's face. The sight chilled her. The woman was up to something, she knew it. Whatever it was, she hoped it wouldn't jeopardize this new and wonderful New Orleans life in any way.

Francis clapped his hands.

"Colleagues! The day is here! We will walk to the bandshell in ten minutes. Please arrive there no later than eleven fifteen, be ready to play at eleven thirty sharp. Music at the ready? Let's go and play well!"

The day was bright. The sun shined from an impossibly lovely sky. Puffy, comfortable-looking white clouds lumbered across the expanse of blue. Melody squinted a bit, but the rush of performance overwhelmed any other sensation, even the warmth of the sun on her shoulders or the smell of the freshly mown grass in the park. The musicians filed along the path.

Angela, the marimba player, struggled to wheel her massive keyboard across a tiny bridge. Melody rushed over and grabbed a corner, smiling at the anxious musician. Angela smiled back.

The walk took just a few minutes, leaving plenty of time for milling about and fussing with sheet music, shuffling chairs, and tuning instruments, and the general pre-performance fidgeting. At 11:20, the group sat silently. Curious onlookers had gathered to watch. Children ran around the grassy expanses behind the benches. Melody watched a young girl chase after a little boy who was chasing a pigeon. At 11:29, Francis strode onto the stage and addressed the crowd.

"Thank you all for being a part of the St. Claire Symphony's inaugural concert. We thank the community of New Orleans for their support and look forward to serving the people of this great city for decades to come."

He turned to the orchestra and raised his hands. Every member brought their instruments to the ready. Francis bobbed his hands once, twice, then began to conduct a well-practiced pattern as familiar to the musicians as their own faces. Melody's first valve was still a bit sticky but was responding adequately enough through the first two pieces.

During the third, it became even more sluggish. It began to affect her playing. Any note that used the first valve was affected by a small glissando. Francis shot her a look. Alarm quickly turned to panic as the valve stuck more and more firmly, each time she pressed it. After a few more messy notes, it wedged itself down entirely.

In a twelve-measure rest, she tried to unstick the valve, but it held firm. She raised the trumpet to her nose and sniffed. Finally, she placed the familiar grade-school project smell.

Epoxy.

She stared at the back of Chelsea's head, wheels turning. She had no proof, but she was sure it was her. Francis looked right at Melody, and she tipped up her trumpet so he could see the stuck valve. His eyes widened, but he didn't miss a beat.

Work with it, he mouthed.

Ten measures later, it was almost time for Melody to play again. She steadied her nerves with a slow, deep breath in, then began to play. She translated the music on the fly, adjusting the notes to fit with the music and to also allow for her to play with the first valve glued shut. It was part improvisation, part mathematical adjustment, part artistic styling. She felt a wave of confusion rumble through the orchestra, but she hoped beyond hope that it was imperceptible to the audience. Maybe her colleagues thought she was showboating, maybe they thought there was some change to her parts they were unaware of, but they rolled with it. The piece ended, everyone settled their instruments down, and Francis turned to the crowd to explain the next musical selection. A few members of the orchestra glanced at Melody without turning their heads. She tried to unstick the valve, but she knew it was futile at this point. There was a rustling of paper as the musicians flipped to their next piece. Her stomach dropped.

She had a solo.

CHAPTER SIXTEEN

As he turned back to the orchestra, Francis shot her a questioning look. She calmly, and she hoped casually, held her horn up enough that he could see the stubbornly stuck valve. His eyebrows lifted, and he nodded. *Do what you can,* he mouthed. She nodded her head almost imperceptibly, and Francis looked at the whole of the orchestra, baton at the ready. He glanced at Melody. Her mother's voice rang in her mind. *Get it together, Red.* She raised her horn to her lips and began to play.

Her solo was bolstered by the entire brass section. She adjusted the music to fit her stuck valve, going up an octave to wail nearly impossibly high notes, dropping into a different but complimentary key for other phrases. Her improvisation sparked a new energy in the group. Everyone's parts were brighter, more invigorated. Toes tapped, and Francis's hair flopped wildly as he conducted with abandon.

The crowd changed. They went from sedately nodding their heads to dancing in the aisles. Kids dragged their grandparents to their feet to jam to the music, couples danced as if they were meeting for the first time, falling in love all over again. Solo dancers danced with love for themselves and the whole world.

Melody focused on the notes written on the page, wildly swerving from measure to measure, jumping from note to note as if she'd been practicing these phrases for months. The rest of the orchestra kept playing impeccably, their musical cues intact. She hoped that Francis's unconcerned face reassured them that it was not an issue. The notes felt more ferociously alive than they'd ever been in the rehearsal room.

As abruptly as the music began, it ended. The crowd, already on their feet, erupted into a cheer so loud that a police cruiser four blocks away swerved back toward them to check on the source of the noise. The orchestra stood, bowed, and smiled.

Francis shook hands and spoke with members of the audience. The orchestra walked back toward the practice hall. Melody hung back, hoping nobody would speak to her. Of course, that was an impossibility—everyone wanted to know what happened. She was instantly mobbed, all of them walking slowly toward the hall. Everyone was abuzz.

"What was that, cher?" asked Renny, concerned.

She held up her horn, the first valve still wedged shut.

"You oiled it, no?" he asked, horrified.

"I did," she said grimly.

A few of their fellow brass players nodded knowingly. They'd all had equipment malfunctions. A few clapped her on the back and told her she'd adjusted well, that she'd played great, that it was a fantastic concert, nonetheless. The crowd quickly dispersed, everyone thrilled to get back, change, and celebrate the successful unveiling of the orchestra.

Melody slowed her pace even more. She leaned close to Renny, held out her horn, and whispered, "Smell it?"

He looked at her curiously but dutifully sniffed the trumpet. His eyes went wide. "Glue?" he said, incredulous.

She nodded.

"I think so," Melody said. "Some kind of epoxy, I'd guess. It got tackier with every movement."

"Tackier than you already are? Unlikely," said a snide voice.

Melody and Renny looked up. Chelsea stood in front of

them, looking imperious and vaguely dangerous in her immaculate black blouse and tailored black pants.

"It was you," Melody said. It wasn't a question. It was a flat statement of fact.

Chelsea held a long-fingered hand to her chest. "Me?" she asked, wide-eyed. "Why, that's quite an accusation. I hope you have something behind that claim. Why would I ever do such a thing?"

Melody's eyes filled with tears. "Why *would* you?" she asked. "How could you? Don't you care about this orchestra at all? You could have ruined the performance!"

Chelsea leaned close to Melody and Renny. "You'd best not make accusations with no proof," she whispered. "It might make you look *cheap* and like a filthy, little liar."

Melody was shocked.

"Did you deliberately sabotage Melody's horn?" asked Renny, his hands shaking.

"Of course not, don't be silly," she said, looking down her nose. "I'm sure that it was musician error, not deliberate shenanigans. Honestly, Melody, it's not like you're experienced. With performing music, that is."

The tumblers in Melody's mind were lining up, falling into place one by one. The hostility from Chelsea, the increase in anger the closer she got to Phillip. Phillip's reluctance to discuss his former relationships in any detail. His subtle insistence on discretion.

"You and Phillip . . ." she mumbled.

Chelsea glared at her.

"Don't even say it. You know nothing, you little interloper. This is not your city. This is not your orchestra, and he is *not* your man."

Renny stepped forward. "Now you wait a minute, Chelsea," he began.

"Is there a problem here?" said a booming voice from

behind them. They all turned to see Francis standing there, with Phillip. Anna was next to them, hands on her hips, glaring at all of them. Francis looked from Chelsea to Melody to Renny. A few of the concertgoers were still in the park and looked curiously at the group of musicians.

"We can continue this conversation elsewhere, perhaps out of public view, no?" Francis said, in a much softer voice.

The group trooped across the park in awkward silence. Melody felt the heat in her face and knew she was so red she might be bordering on purple. Normally, the presence of Phillip would calm her nerves, but she kept glancing at him from the corner of her eye and wondering what else he'd been keeping from her. Chelsea kept her head high, her chin tilted upwards as if the entire world was beneath her. The wheels of her cello case clicked over every groove in the pavement, rolling out an imperfect staccato rhythm.

Chelsea wanted to scream. This was not how she'd imagined this playing out. She reminded herself there was no proof she'd tampered with the trumpet strumpet's instrument. There was nothing they can do to her. After that ridiculous performance, surely, they'd fire Melody for incompetence. Although she did do quite an entertaining job, Chelsea thought begrudgingly. She took solace in that half of the group thought she'd just been showboating, if she could judge by the chatter she'd overheard. Well, at least three people. Well, at least one person talking to two others.

Even as she turned it over in her mind, she knew Melody being unceremoniously fired was not how this would go forward. Melody had done an admirable job adjusting to the sabotaged horn. Marvelous, actually. Chelsea had to hand it to her. She was creative. She wasn't sure she'd have been able to adjust so quickly or with so much panache.

Panache or not, she was sure Francis couldn't let that kind of spontaneity go unaddressed.

Chelsea noticed that Anna, for some reason, was scowling at the ground with a ferocity that she'd never seen from the generally levelheaded woman. She'd seen her snippy and nervous, but never actually angry. A nagging doubt crept into Chelsea's mind. *What if they find out it was me?*

There's no proof. I made sure of that.

Francis entered the building first and strode directly to his office. He didn't look back to see if they were following.

Anna put her hand on Renny's shoulder. "Did you have any part in this?" she asked.

"Naw, ma'am," he said.

She nodded. "I thought not. You can go."

He looked at Melody, who glanced his way with a combination of desperation and sadness. Renny reached out and squeezed Melody's hand, then turned his gaze to Chelsea, imperious as ever, then to Phillip, who looked like he was absolutely miserable. He clapped Melody on the shoulder, then turned and rushed away.

They filed into Francis's office. He sat behind his untidy desk, and sheet music was heaped on every horizontal surface. Everyone else remained on their feet. Anna stood in the corner with her arms folded, looking cross. Francis gazed appraisingly at each of the musicians.

Melody felt like she was a teenager again, called into the principal's office or what she'd imagine that would have felt like. She had never done anything that warranted being called into the principal's office.

Anna spoke first. "What happened out there, Melody?"

"My first valve started sticking during Mon Chante, then stayed stuck all the way down for the last two songs," she answered. She tried not to look at anyone but Anna and reminded herself that she'd done nothing wrong.

"You recovered well," Francis said. "It was a fair bit more allegro than what we practiced, but I suppose that it was far better than you storming away in tears."

"Excuse me, first let me say that I agree that Melody did a wonderful job with her broken horn, but, well, why I am I here?" asked Chelsea.

Anna's nostrils flared, but she looked at Phillip, not Chelsea.

"You're here because your former relationship with Phillip makes us suspect that you tampered with another musician's equipment," said Anna flatly. She was still staring at Phillip, who was staring at the wall behind Francis.

"Excuse me?" Chelsea asked. "I would hardly call anything I do in my free time your business."

Francis slammed his palms on the desk. Everyone jumped.

"Anything that affects this endeavor is our business, Chelsea," he retorted.

"It did not affect this . . ."

"Don't lie to us," Anna said calmly.

"I will not stand here and be accused of some sort of treachery. How dare you?"

Chelsea flipped her hair and jutted out her jaw, but Melody saw her hand was shaking, just a tiny bit.

"Melody, may I see your instrument?" Francis asked. She handed it over. He turned it in his hands, prodded the stuck valve, unscrewed the bottom with some effort, pried the cap off, and inspected it.

"Some kind of adhesive?" he said. He looked at Chelsea. "If this was you, you must tell us now. If we find out later it was you, you will not only be expelled from this orchestra, we will press criminal vandalism charges, as well as make every musical organization in this country aware of your questionable morals."

"When you find the true culprit, I will expect a full apology," said Chelsea. "May I go now?"

Francis looked at her for a long moment. The air in the room roiled with barely suppressed emotion.

"You may," he said.

When the door clicked shut behind her, Anna turned to Phillip.

"I told you to keep your personal life out of this orchestra," she snapped.

Melody thought she might be sick. This was so much a pattern of Phillip's that he'd been warned by the orchestra's director? How many other women had he swept off their feet, only to be discarded when some pretty new musician joined whatever group he was a part of? Had everything been a lie? Had the morning light touching his cheek and making her heart melt been a facade? Had their moments of passion been less special than she'd thought?

"Do . . . do I need to be here?" asked Melody.

Anna crossed her arms. "Phillip? Does she know?"

Phillip flinched.

Melody watched him determinedly staring at the wall. *Look at me.*

He continued to stare ahead, looking beaten.

"I'm sorry."

"Not nearly sorry enough," muttered Francis. "This is a fine pickle you've got us into, son."

Heat washed over Melody, and the room spun. "I think I need to sit . . ." she mumbled, her knees going weak.

Phillip caught her as her legs gave out. She swatted at him but was so dizzy she had no choice but to fall into his arms. God help her, being in his arms felt like going home.

"I never thought she'd hurt you," he whispered to Melody, his gaze locked onto hers.

Tears flowed down her cheeks. This was supposed to have been such a happy day, her first performance as a professional musician. It was all falling apart. Her new relationship, her job, any semblance of respectability. Half the orchestra must think her an egomaniac, the other half, incompetent.

What did she think of herself? She wondered. She had taken a terrible situation and played around it. It was nearly impossible to do what she'd done, and she wasn't blind. She saw the people dancing and cheering. Even if her fellow musicians thought she'd been showboating, the truth would come out. They'd know she'd done her best, and that was what was important. Phillip knew she'd done her best. Phillip knew.

She pushed him away from her. "What aren't you telling me?" she demanded.

He looked sheepish and sad. He ran his hand through his thick dark hair, and Melody couldn't help but swallow. What had he known that might have jeopardized her career? What had he done?

"Chelsea and I have . . . a history," he said.

Anna snorted. "Not exactly ancient now, is it?" Anna scoffed.

Phillip turned to face her, his cheeks red with anger. "You told me it was a bad idea. You were right. Are you happy? I tried to break it off a few times."

"Break what off? How involved were you with her when we got together?" Melody asked.

Francis looked unbearably uncomfortable. "Everyone, please, we need to focus on the matter at hand. Chelsea denies involvement, and we have no proof. Melody, you did an admirable job, considering your instrument malfunction. I have the number of a fantastic brass repair shop, and in appreciation of your performance, I will pay for any necessary repairs. Unless there has been some explicit threat, or you have some evidence of intentional sabotage, this matter is now closed. Please give me your trumpet, and I'll update you after I visit the shop tomorrow."

Melody walked out of the office feeling utterly naked without her instrument. Her emotions also felt too exposed and vulnerable. Phillip walked next to her and tried to speak to her, but Melody could barely hear him. Her mind was swirling with the conversation in Francis's office. Of course, she knew someone as skilled a lover as Phillip was experienced, but it hadn't occurred to her that he would be in the middle of a sticky web of love entanglements.

CHAPTER SEVENTEEN

In a daze, she unlocked the door, and they entered her little house. It had looked cozy and comfortable when they'd left that morning. Now it looked cramped and disheveled. She tossed her purse onto the table, sat down in the rickety chair next to it, and lowered her head in her hands.

Phillip sat in the chair across from her, the legs scraping against the floor and the sound fraying Melody's already raw nerves. She sighed heavily, placed her hands flat on the table in front of her, and looked at Phillip with her stinging, tear-filled eyes.

"Tell me everything," she said. "I need to know the truth."

Phillip reached out to take her hand, but she withdrew it. "No," she said. "I need to hear it all first."

He frowned. "There isn't that much to hear. We were friends since college days, then recently found ourselves both single, so we . . ." His throat bobbed as he swallowed, hard. Melody stared blankly at him. " . . . we started to sleep together."

Melody narrowed her eyes. "How long ago?"

"What do you mean?" he said.

"How long ago did it start, and how long ago did it end? Or did it ever actually end?"

"It ended! I told her a few weeks ago."

Melody slammed her hands on the table. The sudden sound startled Phillip, and the tingling of the impact made her hands feel alive. She could feel a rage building, a slow-burning ferocity like a bursting dam. She'd trusted him, and he was not worthy of that trust. Worse yet, the thrill of falling in love so fast and hard was replaced by a sickening sense of cheapness. She had thought they had something magical, but it was just another day for him. She was just another woman, nothing special.

"A few weeks? We've been together a few weeks. Did you end it before or after that first night in your car?"

"Before! I've been telling her it's over for months, but—"

"Oh, right, because you're just so attractive, she won't let it go?"

Phillip looked down at his hands. Melody felt like she'd slapped him, but the flood of anger wasn't ebbing.

"You couldn't even properly end it with her, then you just draw me into your drama without so much as a word of warning. I spent hours telling you how confused I was by how mean she was being, and you didn't say a damned word!"

He opened his mouth, then closed it again.

"Don't you make that fish face at me!"

He reached for her shoulders. "Melody, I can—"

She swatted his hands away. "You need to leave."

"But—"

"I need you to leave, Phillip."

He stood, looking beaten. "I'm not giving up on us, Melody. We have something special, and I won't just let that go because of a jealous ex."

"You aren't the only one with a say in this." Melody stood. "I'll lock the door after you."

She followed him to the door, and he stepped out. At the last moment, he turned to say something to her, but she slammed the door.

Melody lay on her bed, staring at the ceiling, thoroughly

miserable. Fat tears leaked from the sides of her eyes and down her temples, but she wasn't sobbing. She wished she'd never come to New Orleans. She wished she'd tried out for the New Orleans Philharmonic, where she imagined there was less drama and more professionalism. She wished that Chelsea was . . . what? Less mean? Definitely. Less of a reality in Phillip's life? Maybe. Less threatening? Was that it?

Rolling onto her side, she curled into a ball. Some psychological scar had just been ripped open. Chelsea was an impossibly beautiful and classy Southern belle. Melody was just a short, chunky brass player from Cleveland, but the entire time she'd been with Phillip, she'd felt right. Perfect. Completely free from lacking anything. He'd swept away all of her self-doubts, made her believe she was enough, just as she was.

She certainly didn't feel that way right then.

Tears coursed from her eyes. How had Phillip never even mentioned he was the reason Chelsea was so rude to her? Had he not trusted her? Was he just that self-absorbed that it never occurred to him that his actions were affecting Melody, not just in their romantic life but in her professional life as well?

Melody became aware of a faint mewling. She bolted upright on the bed, the last few self-pitying tears rolling down her cheeks. Wiping them away impatiently, she sat silent and waited. There it was again!

She stood slowly, moved as gently as she could across the room. The sound came a little louder this time, definitely a meow, and it was followed by a rustle outside her window. She stepped quietly out the back door and peeked into the foliage behind her little house at a scrawny black kitten, its eyes shining bright green. It staggered with a paw held tight to its torso, tangled in a six-pack ring. Lord knew how it had got wrapped up in it. She rushed back into the house, grabbed a can of tuna, the can opener, and some scissors, then hurried back outside. She sat on the stair, opened the tuna, and placed it as quietly as she could in front of the kitten's hiding place.

The kitten sniffed at the air, then limped forward, keeping a wary eye on Melody.

"Come on, kitty, kitty," she whispered. It stopped short.

Melody moved back slowly, nudging the tuna forward with her foot. The kitten staggered toward it, and with one more suspicious glare at Melody, began to scarf down the fish. Melody crept toward it, and before it could try to run away, she grabbed it by its scruff. It kicked its legs feebly but had obviously had a hard time of life lately and was very weak. Melody snipped the plastic, and the kitten mewed as its leg dropped free.

She set it gently onto the ground, and it took a few tentative steps. It still limped a bit, but Melody could hear its purrs. It scrambled to the tuna, took a few more bites, then ran back to Melody and rubbed itself against her legs. When it rushed back to eat more, Melody settled on the stoop.

The kitten came back, and Melody held out a hand. The cat rubbed its face against her hand, and Melody smiled. She scratched behind its ears, and it purred so loudly Melody was sure it would rumble itself hoarse.

Suddenly exhausted, Melody stood. She scooped up the little kitten, who nestled into her arm like it had lived with her for its whole life. They went inside. Melody locked the doors, put out a cardboard box with a towel in it for the kitten, and lay on her bed. She was sound asleep in minutes.

CHAPTER EIGHTEEN

The morning light struck Melody in the face, and she groaned. A loud gravelly purr approached, punctuated by a high-pitched meow. Despite her headache and fatigue, Melody smiled at the fast-approaching kitten.

"What's your name, little guy? Are you a guy or . . ." She held up the kitten and looked at its underside. "Yup, little guy."

The kitten purred.

"How about Rachmaninov? You're all rumbly, like one of his piano pieces."

The kitten rumbled, then mewed.

"Okay, Rocky for short?"

He nudged her hand with his tiny face, and warmth spread through her chest. She smiled and set Rocky on the floor. He circled her legs and batted at a balled-up sock.

They headed into the kitchen, and Melody poured herself some cereal. She splashed milk into her bowl and some into a smaller bowl for Rocky. He circled her feet excitedly and lapped at the milk greedily the second she set it down. She patted him and settled into her rickety kitchen table with her breakfast.

She was struck by the moment of happiness. After last night's distress, it was a welcome relief. The day was open, and she couldn't practice even if she wanted to. Her horn was in the shop. Renny had invited her to lunch and on a walking tour to point out a few more haunted buildings in the French Quarter. Her phone buzzed. She glanced at it, and a knot formed in her stomach.

Can we talk? read the text from Phillip.

She stared at it and chewed her cereal. Rocky galloped from one end of her house to the other, chasing a bug. Could they talk? She wasn't sure. On one hand, he'd lied to her by omission. His lack of honesty had made her a fool, one that had unwittingly antagonized Chelsea. On the other hand, she had never felt this way about anyone. Her stomach clenched. She pushed her bowl of cereal away. Rocky hopped onto the table and stuck his face into her bowl, lapping at the leftover milk. She shooed him away gently, then put the bowl on the floor for him.

"Little street urchin," she mumbled, then picked up her phone and dialed.

It rang once.

"Melody! Good morning!" said Phillip. His voice sounded falsely chipper, strained.

"I have until eleven thirty," said Melody. "Do you want to talk in person, or on the phone?"

"I'll be there in fifteen minutes."

She hung up. The clock read 8:45. Shoot. She should have told him she had less time. It seemed like ages ago that she'd ever have wanted to avoid spending time with him, but here they were. Her anger simmered, magma-hot rage ebbing and flowing over rationality. He hadn't sabotaged her, really. He hadn't done anything except have a past that almost cost her a career.

A very recent past, she thought bitterly.

She jumped up and padded into the bathroom. She showered quickly, with Rocky pacing on the other side of the shower curtain. When she was toweling off, he jumped in to inspect the tub, batting at water droplets dripping from the faucet. She walked out and got dressed, casual in a tank top and shorts that showed off her curves without being an overt invitation. She looked at herself in the mirror, her face a little puffy from last night's crying jag. She shrugged. Nothing to be done for that now.

There was a knock on the door. Rocky sprinted to a box and tucked himself inside, his green eyes glinting from the back corner. Melody steeled herself and walked to the door.

Phillip stood on the other side. Dark circles ringed his brown eyes, and today they were filled with anguish more than their usual warmth. The moment Melody opened the door, she wanted nothing more than to collect him in her arms and kiss him until he wasn't upset anymore. The thing she wanted second most, and would always want, was to be in a relationship with honesty and integrity at its core. She stifled that momentary urge to stroke his hair and tell him it would all be okay. She wrapped her arms around herself.

"May . . . may I come in?" he asked.

It was the first time he'd asked to enter. Normally their mouths were busy kissing, or she was pulling him through the door. This time, she merely nodded and stepped to the side. A tiny hiss emanated from the box where Rocky was hiding.

"Did you get a cat?" he asked, astounded.

She nodded. "He showed up on my doorstep a hot mess, and I helped him. Named him Rocky."

Phillip knelt next to the box and peeked inside. He smiled. Rocky swiped a paw at him.

"I don't think he likes you," said Melody, her arms still folded.

Phillip stood. The cat darted from the box and circled Melody's feet. She bent down and scooped him up. He immediately started to purr.

"Likes you, though," Phillip said. "Smart cat."

"What did you want to talk about?" Melody asked, her voice flat and resigned.

"Yesterday," Phillip said. "And today and tomorrow, and all the days after."

"That's quite a lot of conversation," she said. "I guess we should have some coffee."

Melody sat down at the kitchen table. Phillip sat across from her. Even through the swirl of emotions in her chest, she still felt drawn to his perfectly arched lips, his sharp nose, and the dark stubble along his chin. Tears sprang to her eyes. Why did he have to be so . . . what? Not quite dishonest. Not quite truthful. Unforthcoming? Was that a word? She stared at him silently.

"I'm sorry I didn't tell you about Chelsea," he said. "I thought it would make it more awkward for you."

"For me? Or for you?" she asked.

He looked at his hands.

"I thought for you, but it wasn't entirely altruistic, I suppose," he said.

She nodded and scowled. He reached his hands toward her. She relaxed her arms and allowed him to take her hands. The second he touched her, she felt something unwind in her chest, and a warm honeyed rush move through her stomach. Tears threatened to spill from her eyes.

"I want to trust you," she said.

"You can."

"How? You didn't even trust me with your past."

He gripped her hands, firm but gentle. She could feel his pulse or hers. A tear rolled down her cheek.

"I will tell you anything you want to know," he said.

"Okay," she mumbled. "Did you love her?"

"Not romantically. We've been friends for so long, I've never thought of it as love. More, familiarity."

"Does she love you?"

He paused.

Melody's stomach clenched, but she couldn't help but be

impressed that he seemed to be taking the question seriously.

"I think she just wants me to be hers," he said. "It's not so much love as it is possessiveness."

Melody nodded. "I can see that. That makes a lot of sense as to why she'd lash out at me. Do you think she's done now?"

"Yes," he said, but his hands tensed.

She believed him anyway.

Melody moved Rocky to the floor and stood. She took Phillip's hand and drew him to his feet. She wrapped her arms around him and pressed herself against him. She drew in a hitching breath as he slid his arms over her shoulders. He rubbed her, moving a hand lower, to the small of her back, and slid his fingers under her shirt. She looked up at him and put her hand on his cheek, reveling in the stubble beneath her fingers. He leaned down and kissed her. She parted her lips, and his tongue found hers. She ran her hand through his hair, and he slid his hands down, over her buttocks, lifting her hips so he could kiss her more easily.

She sighed, felt him press against her. She could feel the outline of his bulge between her legs, and a wave of heat rolled through her. He carried her to the bedroom and set her down onto the bed.

"Is this okay?" he asked.

In answer, she took his face in her hands and kissed him gently. She reclined, and he laid down next to her.

"I will never lie to you again," he said, "by omission or otherwise."

She rolled onto him, straddling him. She peeled off her tank top. Phillip slid his hands up her sides and ran the tips of his fingers under the lace band of her bra. He moved toward the clasp on the back, unhooked it deftly and drew it down off her shoulders. Her nipples rose as the morning air touched them. She shuddered as Phillip ran his hands over them, the callouses from his violin playing rough against her tender breasts.

She arched her back and slid her shorts from her legs. His eyes were locked with hers as he lifted his shirt. She sat up and reached for his taut abs, running her fingers down the line of hair on his stomach to the front of his jeans. It tickled her finger, smooth and rough at the same time. She undid the button and zipper, then peeled his pants and undershorts down with one smooth motion. He kicked them off as he stepped forward. She slid back onto the bed, onto her back, and he followed her. She parted her legs, and he moved to her, kissing her, his hand moving from her breast to her stomach to her cleft.

He gently drew circles around her clitoris, and she moaned with pleasure. She was ready for him, and he didn't wait one more second. He parted her lips gently and slid the length of himself into her. She gasped, as always, shuddering as he filled her. He rocked his hips back, and she rolled with his movements. He drew himself almost entirely out of her, then slowly and gently slid back in.

It felt so good and so right.

Melody wrapped her legs around him, keeping him inside of her. She began to rock against him, her pleasure building. She crested like a wave, her orgasm wrenching a cry from her throat. With a moan, Phillip released his orgasm into her.

"Melody, I love you!" he gasped.

They lay together, panting, exhausted, and both smiling.

"I love you too."

She ran a hand over his muscular chest. "It's good to have a day off."

He drew her closer to him, and though the day was already warm and the air humid, she snuggled into the curve of his body, smiling.

CHAPTER NINETEEN

The next morning, the two of them arrived for rehearsal together. As soon as she walked into his office, Francis handed the case containing her newly repaired trumpet and smiled.

"It was a simple fix," he said. "Your saboteur put a small bit of epoxy glue into your valve, but the felt kept it from spreading. The repair shop simply used mineral spirits to loosen and clean the adhesive, then replaced the felt and the spring for good measure."

He handed her the case, and she almost wept with relief.

"It's not messed up?"

Francis smiled kindly. "No, dear, it is most decidedly not *messed up*."

Melody practically skipped to her seat, and Renny leaned forward to whisper in her ear, "Looks like y'all figured your stuff out, yeah? Boyfriend and trumpet too?"

She turned and grinned.

He clapped her shoulder, then laughed. "Good on you, cher."

Melody settled into her seat and toyed with her valves, reveling in the pleasure of the smooth movement, unhindered by glue or sabotage. She felt eyes on her and looked up. Chelsea was turned in her seat, staring hard, her look inscrutable. Melody sat up straighter. *I'm not afraid of you.*

As if the dark-haired woman had heard her thoughts, Chelsea shot Melody a quick glare and spun around.

Anna stood prim at the front of the room, watching Chelsea closely. They locked gazes when Chelsea turned to the front.

They have no proof, Chelsea reminded herself, holding the gaze. Anna stared for a moment longer, then walked out of the room. Chelsea let out a breath she hadn't even realized she'd been holding.

The rest of the day passed in a blur for all in the orchestra. All of them were flying high from their recent successful performance, and most had congratulated Melody on her quick recovery. Many thought that some local kids had snuck into the hall somehow and tampered with her instrument. Chelsea's cello swiveled as she kept peeking back at the brass section, then the violins. She grew more upset with every look. Obvious warmth passed between Phillip and Melody, and every smile between them was a dagger in her heart. Her jealousy clawed at her like a ravaging beast. She knew that it was unfair, but how could she have been so smitten with someone who would leave behind his own child?

Yes, it was a child that didn't exist except in a lie, but how could Phillip know that? He'd thrown Chelsea's past in her face, the lie she'd told to an ex, the same lie she told Phillip, but he couldn't be sure. What a terrible man who would run out on his child. The jealousy turned a corner, changed and morphed into something else, something darker and more awful. She started to loathe Phillip. She no longer wanted to win his affection. She wanted to bring him down.

Her bow hit a sour note, and Francis brought the orchestra to a screeching cut.

"Chelsea, that phrase was beneath your talents," he snarled.

"Beneath my talents?" she repeated. "This whole orchestra is beneath my talents."

One of the percussionists gasped. The rest of the room was

dead still until a voice shattered the silence.

"Maybe you should leave, then," Melody said.

Chelsea spun to face her. Heat rose in her face. She held herself very still so she wouldn't launch herself over the two rows of musicians between them and claw out Melody's eyes. The bassoon player in front of Melody shrank behind her instrument. Everyone's eyes were on Chelsea.

Fine. I'll show you, little bitch.

Chelsea turned on her heel and stormed out, leaving her cello propped against her chair. A murmur ran through the room. All eyes flitted between Melody, who stood, shaking in front of her chair clutching her trumpet, and Francis, who stood at his podium looking baffled.

A moment later, the sound of squealing tires shrieked from the parking lot and a loudly revved engine sped away.

Melody sat down, trembling. She took a deep breath to try to steady herself. Renny leaned forward and gave her shoulder a squeeze she barely felt. Her mind spun. Had she really just chased away the cello darling of New Orleans? Her gaze caught on Chelsea's abandoned cello like a shirt catching on a nail and seemed stuck there once she'd noticed it. She hadn't even put it in a case. She didn't even take it with her.

"Rhiannon, practice the solo in Fleur de Lis," Francis said calmly. Rhiannon, the second-chair cellist, nodded somberly. A few of the cellists looked pleased. *Maybe I wasn't the only one she was so rude to.* She tore her focus from the cello section and looked at Phillip. He was staring at the lonely cello, his brows furrowed.

Phillip had never seen her like that, in all the years they'd known each other. Was this how unhinged she'd seemed to Henri when he'd found out she'd lied about being pregnant?

He thought back to that time, but he hadn't really known Henri. He hadn't ever known Chelsea when she was seeing someone. Now that he thought about it, she was single when they were friends. His stomach clenched. It was a terrible mistake to get involved with her, he saw that now. As sure as he was that she was not pregnant with his child, if it turned out she was, he would have a lifetime tied to her, her tantrums, and her lies.

He had felt so fondly for her a few short weeks earlier. Now, all he could think of was Melody. His feelings for Chelsea seemed empty and brittle, crumbling the more he examined them in the bright light of his love for Melody. He looked at her, copper curls illuminated by the early afternoon light. His shoulders relaxed immediately. He realized that Francis had been speaking for a few minutes.

" . . . behavior is not becoming of the professional image of the St. Claire Symphony, and we are far too nascent to be known for this level of dramatics. Should anyone consider emulating Ms. Carr's outburst, I strongly suggest you reconsider. We shall return her cello, but she shall not return to this organization. Now, let's attempt to play Les Bon Temps once more, and put today's ugliness behind us."

He raised his baton, and all of them sat up, instruments at the ready. They played through the piece. Though they were all distracted by the drama and a fleet of sirens that wailed past their windows during the allegro, it went well enough to satisfy Francis.

He ran them through a few more of their performance pieces, the day fading away as they filled the room with harmonies and musical moods. At long last, Francis tapped the podium to gather their attention to him.

"That is enough for today," he said. "Well done, but practice the allegro in Bon Temps for tomorrow's rehearsal. It could be much . . ."

He trailed off as Anna burst into the room. She rushed to the podium and whispered something into Francis's ear. He looked at Phillip, then the group. A chill ran down Phillip's spine. Something was very wrong.

"Good work today. Dismissed," he said and hurried out of the room. Anna looked at Phillip and pointed at him. Without a word, Phillip scrambled to his feet and followed.

Melody sat in her chair, paralyzed by warring curiosity and caution. Whatever had happened probably had nothing to do with her, but she couldn't help but feel involved. Phillip was obviously involved. Did it have something to do with Chelsea? With this much drama? It seemed likely.

She stood, unsteady on her feet. She walked to the door of Francis's office. She stood outside, listening. The words were faint on the other side of the door and were partially drowned out by the rest of the orchestra leaving. Melody's skin crawled at her reckless intrusion into their conversation, but she *had* to know. As the last musicians left, she could finally make out more words.

" . . . she told me she was pregnant," she heard Phillip's voice say.

The world stopped spinning. Melody's face went numb. Her legs turned to jelly, and she slid to the floor. Through a warped soundscape, snippets of conversation wobbled to her ears.

" . . . it wasn't true, because she'd lied before . . ."

" . . . involved with multiple members of the orchestra . . ."

" . . . jeopardized everything because of your amorous endeavors . . ."

The words ran together and became meaningless. Melody's chest hurt. She couldn't breathe. Her lungs weren't working, and she feared if she were able to breathe in, she would scream. She wrapped her arms around herself and rocked.

The office door flew open, narrowly missing her foot. Anna stormed out, not noticing Melody. Phillip followed, but he immediately saw her crumpled on the floor. He dropped to his knees beside her.

"Melody. *Melody!* Are you all right?" he exclaimed. He put his arms around her, but she flailed against him. She was finally able to draw a breath, and a sound of pure rage escaped her throat. He wrapped his arms around her, pinning her fists to her sides. Tears streamed down her face. She went slack. Her body trembled.

"Melody!" he said, running a hand over her hair. She shoved him away. He fell backward, shocked.

"Pregnant?" was all she could shout.

The color drained from his face. "How much did you hear?" he asked.

Her jaw dropped. How much did she need to hear? She heard that Chelsea was pregnant. Wasn't that more than enough? "You told me there was nothing else! The whole truth, you said," she sputtered.

"There isn't anything else," he said. "She is not pregnant!"

"Wh . . . what?"

"She pulled this on a boyfriend when she was in her early twenties. Told him she was pregnant to keep him around, but when he found out the truth, he packed up and moved away faster than a cheetah on fire."

"What does that have to do with . . ."

"I do not believe that she is pregnant with my child. I do not believe that she is pregnant at all."

Melody looked at him, disgusted. He looked confident that he had put the matter to rest, that everything was now squared away. She curled her lip, and the look of certainty faded from his face. "What if she is, Phillip? You just discarded her?"

The room was silent. The door creaked open, and Francis entered the hall. He stooped down and groaned as he gracelessly plopped himself onto the floor. His legs stuck out in front of him. He was obviously a man unused to sitting on the floor. "Then that makes this situation doubly difficult," he said. "Melody, there's been an accident."

"Accident?" she said.

Francis nodded, his wispy white hair undulating.

"Chelsea has been in a motor vehicle collision," he said. "She is currently at St. Mary's. Anna has gone to visit her and check her condition, and we will be following her there shortly." He gave Phillip a stern look. "Won't we?"

Phillip stared at the floor. A muscle twitched in his perfect jaw, and despite her emotional distress and frustration with him, Melody had an urge to reach out and rest her hand against his cheek. Could Chelsea be lying? Could Phillip be the good judge of character and the upstanding man she had thought he was? Could she ever trust him again?

"I don't think it's such a good idea for me to go," he said.

"You have to," Melody said. "You have to go and see this through."

Phillip stood, pale and deadly serious. He reached his hand to Francis, who took it gratefully and awkwardly clambered to his feet. Phillip reached his hand to Melody.

"There's nothing to see through," he said. "Even if she is . . . we're over."

She looked at his hand, there in the air. She thought of the moments that hand had run over her skin, the pleasure it had brought her. She felt weak and fragile like she just wanted to go home.

"You should go now," she said bitterly. *Go to her — she won.*

Francis put his hand on Phillip's shoulder and guided him toward the front door. Phillip looked beaten, and Melody felt her heart breaking in her chest. The moment the door closed behind them, she lay on the floor and cried.

For the second time that day, she'd told someone to leave, and they had. She could only hope this time it wouldn't be such a life and death disaster.

CHAPTER TWENTY

The machines beeped steadily around Chelsea's still form. Her delicate features were paler than usual in the harsh hospital lights. Anna sat next to her, gingerly holding Chelsea's hand. An IV line protruded from her arm. Francis and Phillip walked in, but Anna didn't look up.

"They're keeping her in a coma for the time being," she said.

Phillip slipped his palm under Chelsea's. Her motionless hand seemed even more unnaturally still in his shaking one. A woman in scrubs and a white coat walked into the room. A badge clipped to her pocket read Dr. Lieu. She plucked a chart from a plastic pocket on the wall.

"Is there a Phillip Masters here?" she said.

Phillip raised his hand.

"You're listed as her medical proxy," she said. "Can we speak in private?"

"Is that necessary?" he asked. He looked at Chelsea's unconscious face, then at Anna and Francis's concerned ones.

"No," she said, "but it's more respectful to Ms. Carr."

Phillip shook his head. "If you can say it to me, you can say it in front of these two. We are as much family as she's got."

Dr. Lieu frowned. "Fine," she muttered. "I don't have time. Ms. Carr has suffered a great deal of blunt force trauma, but all of her tests signal a very positive prognosis. We're keeping her sedated for the time being, for the next few hours at least, to allow her body to heal some of that trauma."

"What about the baby?" Francis asked.

The doctor's eyebrows shot upwards. She flipped a few pages in the chart. "I wasn't aware she was pregnant," she said. "We'll have the ultrasound redone immediately. The initial scan checked for internal bleeding only."

The doctor strode from the room and picked up a phone across the hallway. She held the receiver to her ear and looked through the doorway at Chelsea, then turned away as she spoke. Phillip sank into a battered green chair next to Chelsea's bed, his hand still under hers. Francis rubbed Anna's shoulders. She cried silently.

"We failed her," said Francis.

Anna stroked Chelsea's hair. Phillip stood awkwardly next to the bed. He didn't want to touch Chelsea, but he felt huge boulders of regret weighing on his shoulders, keeping his hand exactly where it was. If only he hadn't gotten involved with her, if only he'd been more adamant about ending things, if only, if only.

Her pale face seemed to draw the warmth out of his soul. She was lying silent and far too still, her breath slow and shallow.

A man in gray and black scrubs rolled in a cart laden with machinery. He tucked the sheet down around her hips and eased Chelsea's gown up to expose a patch of her abdomen. Phillip cringed at the red welts where the seat belt had dug into her. The ultrasound technician squirted a dollop of gel onto her stomach. He ran the ultrasound transducer through it, and a black and white picture erupted on the screen. The man frowned, moved the transducer to different angles, clicking a key on a keyboard at seemingly random intervals. The picture changed, was still an uninterpretable mass of squiggles to the untrained eye. He looked at everyone in the room, calm and appraising, then set the transducer onto a disposable sheet of paper on the cart.

"I'll be right back," he said. "Please don't touch any of

that."

The three stared at Chelsea, silent.

"That cannot be good," said Francis.

Anna nodded, but Phillip wasn't so sure. He had a suspicion of what the ultrasound technician saw that had upset him—nothing.

Dr. Lieu returned to the room, grim. She pressed a few buttons on the machine and scrolled through the images. As she looked at the screen, she leaned closer until her nose was almost touching the monitor. Her hand moved impossibly fast, clicking to bring up picture after picture. Anna and Francis watched with concern, but Phillip could only sit back in his chair and feel an uncomfortable combination of relief and distress. Relief that he'd been right, that Chelsea wasn't pregnant, and distress that he'd been so blind to her manipulative nature. He'd known she'd had it in her after she'd told him that she'd tried this exact thing with an ex. For some reason, he thought they'd had a more honest relationship or fling, whatever you'd call it.

When someone shows you who they are, believe them the first time. Maya Angelou was right.

Dr. Lieu strode to the bed and picked up the nurse call button. She pressed it, and moments later a harried-looking woman in cartoon-print scrubs rushed in. When she saw Dr. Lieu holding the button she frowned.

"What do you need, doctor?" she asked.

"We need to run an HCG test on this patient, right away please."

"Of course," said the nurse, and she rushed away. Dr. Lieu turned to the trio at Chelsea's bedside.

"We have to run another test to determine her pregnancy's status," she said. "It will be a few hours before we get the results from the lab."

"Is the baby hurt?" asked Anna, concerned. Dr. Lieu looked at her with a steady gaze.

"I'll let you know as soon as I get the test results," she said. "You're welcome to wait if you'd like, but I can just as easily call."

"We'll wait," said Anna firmly. "We're as close to a family as she has."

"You aren't her parents?" asked the doctor. Anna and Francis exchanged a look.

"Of course, we are," said Francis, putting his hand on Anna's shoulder. "My wife is very upset and misspoke, obviously. We are the *closest* family she has."

Dr. Lieu didn't look entirely convinced but let it drop.

Phillip stood. "Does anyone want anything from the commissary?" he asked.

"Coffee, please," said Francis.

Anna shook her head. She didn't even look at Phillip, and her determined avoidance of looking at him upset him. He could read the disapproval on her face as clearly as if it were tattooed there in capital letters.

"I'll be back as soon as I have the lab results, then," Dr. Lieu said and left them alone.

Phillip started to leave the room, but Francis reached out and put a hand on his arm. He squeezed. When Phillip met his eyes, he was surprised to see the depth of sadness and compassion he saw there. *I see you,* the look said. *I know this pain.* He touched Francis's hand and walked out. He'd never considered that Francis was ever a man of passion, but this small gesture spoke of some past of pain and lost love. He walked the long hallway toward the cafeteria, the smell of antiseptic sharp in his nose. When all of this was over, he'd have to make a point to get to know a little more about Francis's history.

Phillip wandered around the cafeteria putting random items onto a tray. He paid the cashier and walked slowly back to the room. He set the tray on the rolling table in the room, and Anna and Francis snatched the coffees. He didn't have the energy to say that one was actually for him, that Anna had rejected his offer. Numb, he opened a bottle of apple juice instead and bit into a cold croissant.

The room was quiet, save for the beeping of the machines and general hospital chatter floating in from the hallway. The three sat in silence, staring at their fallen cellist, while the minutes ticked by, turning into hours. Phillip occasionally looked at his phone, hoping for a message from Melody. Nothing came through.

Four hours later, Francis sat snoozing in his chair, and Phillip was crafting the fifth revision of a text apology to Melody. Anna was quietly sipping a fresh coffee. Dr. Lieu strode into the room, and Phillip leaped to his feet.

"I'm sorry to tell you this, but Chelsea is not pregnant," she said.

Anna gasped and began to cry. "She lost the baby!" she wailed.

Dr. Lieu looked at her flatly. "I want to be clear, ma'am. This was not a case of her losing the baby in the collision. She has not recently been pregnant."

Francis looked at Phillip, who nodded gravely.

Anna looked from the doctor to Chelsea. "She was lying?"

Francis put his hand on Anna's arm.

She shrugged it off angrily and stormed from the room.

Dr. Lieu looked mildly uncomfortable. "I'm afraid there's not much more I can offer to you today," she said. "If you'd like to speak with someone in our psychological counseling services, I could set that up."

Francis shook his head. "We are fine. Thank you, doctor. We have got a fair bit to chew on for the time being, and we appreciate all of your help."

She nodded curtly and left the room. Francis and Phillip were left in awkward silence.

"I suppose someone should stay with her for now," said Francis. "I'll take the first shift, but please promise me that you'll come back."

"For you, Francis."

The older man smiled sadly.

"Go to her," he said.

Phillip did.

CHAPTER TWENTY-ONE

Melody smoothed tape onto the slightly battered cardboard box. Rocky darted around next to her, chewing a bit of newspaper here and jumping into a box there. She watched his antics, wondering what it would feel like to be so carefree. The box was put together, ready to be filled with her belongings, so she tossed it into the stack. It fell over onto its side and had barely landed when Rocky launched himself into it. Melody wiped away a tear.

The doorbell rang. She wiped her brow and walked to the door. Phillip stood on her stoop, his eyes tired and his face familiar, beautiful, and heartbreaking. She turned and walked back inside, leaving the door open.

"Close it after you," she said.

"Southern manners would dictate that, of course, ma'am," he said, smiling. She didn't return his smile.

She crossed her arms.

"What is it?" she said.

"What's going on in here?" he asked.

"Moving," she said.

He bent down to scoop up Rocky into his big, graceful hands. The kitten hissed, then nibbled his thumb, then cuddled into his elbow. Melody wanted Phillip to go. Seeing him was too painful. She wished she could stop seeing him as a man who cared for kittens or who cared for her. After all, he'd jeopardized her career by not telling her about Chelsea's vendetta against her and jeopardized her heart by not being honest. What kind of man leaves a pregnant woman?

"Where to?" he said.

"Home," she said and burst into tears. He set Rocky down and walked to her, put his arms around her. She sobbed harder and pushed him away. She struck his chest with a balled-up fist, but her punch lacked resolve. "No, you don't get to do that," she said, furious.

"Do what?" he asked, his voice choked with emotion. His arms hung limply at his sides.

She wanted their easy touches back, their casual camaraderie. She hungered for the comfort of his touch but was equally repulsed by him at the moment. "Comfort me," she said. "Love me."

A tear rolled down his perfect chiseled cheek. He smeared it away quickly. "I have to," he whispered. "I love you so much."

She crossed an arm in front of her and wiped at her face angrily. "Then how could you lie to me? How could you walk away from Chelsea when she's going to have your child? What's to say you won't walk away from me?"

"Melody," he said. "Chelsea's not pregnant. We found out at the hospital."

"You just found out, Phillip. You left when you didn't know."

"I did know, Mel." He sat at her kitchen table. The chair squeaked in protest. "She tried this with an ex. I thought because we had kept things casual, somehow, she wouldn't treat me like her exes. Chelsea's always been a tad, well, manipulative."

"You could say that again," Melody muttered.

"I will say it again," he said, his voice getting louder and strained. "I will say it over and over again until you believe me."

"You can't make me love you!" she shouted.

"I don't have to! You already do!" he shouted back.

They stared at each other for a moment, breathing hard. Rocky cowered in a box nearby. Phillip slumped in his chair. Melody sat down across from him.

"Look where that got me," she said, putting her head in her hands.

"You don't have to go," he said. "Please don't go."

She shook her head without looking at him. "I don't know how I can stay," she said.

He reached his hand across the table and stroked Melody's curls. "Please," he said.

Her head tilted, and the weight of it rested in Phillip's hand. As quickly as she'd relaxed, she sat upright. "I need some time," she said. "Please go."

He withdrew his hand and stared at her for a moment, then stood. "I will do whatever I can to make this right," he said.

She looked at him sadly and felt like her heart was breaking all over again. She stood to walk him to the door. "I don't know what that is."

He gathered her into his arms. The tension melted out of her. She felt safe, and loved, and conflicted. She tilted her chin toward him. He leaned in and kissed her, gently. Every fiber of her being wanted to be with him, save the one nagging part of her that said he had lied to her. She tried to stuff that voice down, to let the swirl of emotions drown it out, to let the warm honey flowing in her stomach at his kiss wash it away. It wouldn't hush. She pushed him away, reluctantly.

"I have to think," she said.

"When you're ready, I'm here. I'll wait for you."

She shut the door behind him and collapsed onto the floor. Rocky padded to her and rubbed his face against her knee, purring like a chainsaw. She stroked his fur absently, then stood so suddenly he bolted, startled, into another cardboard box.

Melody grabbed her keys and ran out the door.

CHAPTER TWENTY-TWO

The bus let Melody off just in front of the hospital. She practically sprinted into the building, noticing even in her rush that the building was slick and modern in a way that she hadn't expected. She'd known of the old, beautiful hospital that had been abandoned since Katrina but hadn't thought to consider that New Orleans had other, newer hospitals.

Get over yourself. You don't know everything about this city. It's only been a few months, what did you expect?

The woman at the information desk was helpful and friendly in that particular no-nonsense New Orleans way, directing Melody to the neurology ward. Melody was terrified when the elevator door opened to a beige hallway and the sound of someone crying and another moaning. The nurses rushed around, calm centers in the hurricane of illness around them. Melody's heart pounded. She wasn't sure what she'd expected, but it hadn't been the intimidatingly named Neurology Ward.

She looked for the room number that she'd been given at the front desk. When she found it, she came face-to-face with Anna, who was sitting at Chelsea's bedside. Her eyes were red-rimmed, and she looked exhausted. When she looked up at Melody, those same eyes widened in surprise.

"Melody! I . . . dear . . . it's so sweet of you to come but . . ." She waved her hand at Chelsea's still form. Her body was motionless save for the rhythmic, mechanical rise and fall of her chest.

"Oh, Anna," Melody said. The older woman rushed into

her open arms and sobbed. Melody peeked over her shoulder at Chelsea. She couldn't take her eyes from the tubes connected to Chelsea's body, from the motionless face.

Anna took a few hitching breaths and stood back from Melody. She put her hands on Melody's shoulders and gave them a gentle squeeze.

"Since you're here, would you mind staying for a few minutes? I'd love to get a coffee and snack, but just can't bring myself to leave her alone. The doctors said she will wake soon and, oh, I'm afraid she'd be so scared if no one is here. I just can't bear the thought."

"Of course," she said. "I'll be right here."

Anna gave her one last hug, and Melody settled herself into the chair next to Chelsea's bed. It was still warm from Anna's body. She squirmed, her heart racing. It took a few moments for Melody to pinpoint her discomfort. Though Chelsea was unconscious, Melody was still afraid of her. As soon as she acknowledged that fear, though, it faded away. As her anxiety ebbed, she began to see Chelsea differently. Her features changed from sharp and haughty to frail and brittle. Her cruel actions seemed to morph, in retrospect, into desperation.

Melody reached out and slid her hand under Chelsea's. It was cool and limp and seemed full of too many bones.

"I know how you feel, sort of," she said, the comatose woman's hand heavy in hers. Chelsea stayed still and silent.

"I don't know what I'd do if he was leaving me," she said. "I mean, I guess that's exactly what I'm doing. I'm leaving him, but if he left me, for you, I don't know what I'd do."

The machines hummed. Chelsea didn't respond.

"I don't want to go," she said. Her eyes burned, and she blinked back tears. "I want to stay here and be with him, but I don't know how to trust him after all this. I mean, you're pretty awful and manipulative, but he was just going to leave you in the cold when you said you were pregnant. I had to see you. You're the only other woman who knows how I feel right now."

A man in a white lab coat, stethoscope around his neck, walked very slowly past the door. He peeked in the room, and Melody looked at him curiously, wiping her cheeks.

"Doctor?" she called out.

He walked in and held up a hand awkwardly.

"I didn't mean to interrupt," he said. "I'm an old . . . friend. Just wanted to stop and say hi."

"Are you a doctor here?" Melody asked.

"I am. Cardiologist." He tugged at the badge clipped to his lab coat pocket. Henri LeFontaine, MD.

"Anything you can do for a broken heart?" Melody asked, trying to make a joke but betrayed by a quivering lower lip.

"I'm sorry, miss, I'm afraid that's above even my considerable pay grade." He pulled a chair closer to the bed and sat. "Are you close with Chelsea?"

Melody shook her head. "I don't think you'd say that. She tried to sabotage my trumpet because my boyfriend is her ex."

The doctor threw back his head and laughed, then grinned at Chelsea. He had slight dimples and a rather charming smile. He reached forward and stroked Chelsea's forehead, smoothing her dark hair back. There was something so familiar in his touch Melody was sure that there was a long, storied history there.

"Same ol' Chels," he said, fondly.

"I'm sorry, how do you know her?" Melody asked.

"We were lovers," he drawled. "We were so young. Things didn't work out, and it got, well, complicated. I left, finished medical school, threw myself into medicine, but I never really stopped loving her."

"Good luck with that," Melody muttered.

"Sorry?" asked the doctor.

Melody shook her head. "Nothing," she said, eyes filling

with tears once more. "It was literally nothing."

Dr. LeFontaine couldn't shift his focus off of Chelsea. He ran his hand over her forehead, her cheek. Melody was quite certain he wanted to kiss her, but was glad he controlled himself. It was strange enough to watch him caress the unconscious woman's face.

A nurse strode into the room with a clipboard in her hands. She glanced at Dr. LeFontaine and at Melody, then looked at some of the many machines connected to Chelsea.

"Everything looks good," she said. "Except for you being here, Dr. LeFontaine."

"There's nothing improper about my being here, Marnie," he said. "My shift is over for the day."

The nurse shook her head and walked out, making notes on Chelsea's chart.

"What was that about?" asked Melody. She felt a bond with this doctor, the type of bond that only arises by sitting vigil at the bedside of someone, not knowing how they'd fare after they'd healed. Even with his strangeness and his too-familiar touches of Chelsea's face, she could tell he cared deeply for the woman lying in the bed. It made Melody pity him.

"As I said, Chelsea and I have a past. It may not seem like it, but New Orleans is a small town, at its heart," he said. He leaned his forehead onto Chelsea's hand. "I wish I could play music for you, mon cheri."

"Would that help?" asked Melody.

"It may. There have been some promising studies showing that music encourages brain recovery after an injury."

Before he finished speaking, Melody had jumped from her seat and was halfway out the door.

"Stay with her until Anna gets back," she said, "I'll be back as soon as I can."

As she bolted from the room, she heard him say, "Who's Anna?"

She ran from the hospital, the fresh, humid air feeling like a warm hug after the cold sterility of the neurology ward. The bus appeared immediately, almost as if it was summoned by the drama at the hospital. She stared out of the window, watching the streets roll by. French-styled balconies and concrete stoops, immaculate mansions and shotgun houses still damaged from a long-ago flood. As the bus pulled up to the stop in front of her house, she barely waited for it to pause before jumping out.

She rushed inside and grabbed her trumpet case. Rocky meowed loudly and indignantly, and Melody skidded to a stop in front of his food bowl. She dumped some kitten kibble into it, and Rocky crunched it greedily, purring. She ran from the house and back to the bus stop that would take her back to the hospital. Impatiently, she waited.

CHAPTER TWENTY-THREE

By the time Melody returned to Chelsea's bedside, over an hour had passed, and the doctor was gone. Melody barely noticed his absence as she sat down next to the hospital bed. Anna was sitting quietly in the corner, watching Melody with gentle curiosity. Melody bent her head over the case and clicked open the clasps. She smiled at the instrument there, cradled in red velvet and smelling of the sharp, brassy valve oil and polish. With a well-practiced tug, she freed the trumpet from its case.

She wiggled the mute from its strap and tucked it into the bell of the horn. She began to play. The music took on the tinny, melancholy air that a mute lends to brass instruments, but the deep emotion behind every note rang through the room. She played Chet Baker, she played Miles Davis, she played cheerful ragtime and mournful ballads. Time slipped past unnoticed until she paused between songs and someone in the doorway clapped their hands.

Phillip was standing there, illuminated by the light from the hallway. When had the room become dark? She looked out the window and realized the sun had set hours ago.

"Oh, my gosh what time is it?" she asked.

"About time for me to be gone," said Anna. "Good night, you two. Please call me when she awakens. They said it could be any minute about six hours ago."

Phillip nodded solemnly to Anna as he walked in and sat down across from Melody. Anna slipped quietly from the room.

"It's past nine," he said. Melody blinked. She'd grabbed her trumpet sometime in the afternoon. She had been so engrossed with her playing it took her a moment to register the emotions roiling in her upon seeing Phillip. His beautiful face drawn in distress, broad shoulders slumped in sadness. She wanted to run to him and kiss every inch of his face, but she had to hold herself back. She had to leave, didn't she?

"Not bad, trumpet strumpet," said a weak voice from the bed. Melody and Phillip jumped.

"Chelsea!" Phillip said, rushing forward to take her hand. Melody took a step away from her, suddenly afraid.

Phillip leaned close to Chelsea's face and said softly, "I told you that you weren't pregnant."

To Melody's surprise, Chelsea tried to laugh, but it quickly turned from a chuckle into a gasp and coughing. Chelsea rested a hand on her ribcage.

"Shit, they're broken?" she asked.

Phillip nodded.

"What are you guys doing here? I thought you'd have been celebrating my imminent demise."

"Not so imminent, dear," said a stout nurse from the doorway. She walked in and gently guided Phillip away from the bed so she could put a blood pressure cuff on Chelsea's arm. "Good to see you awake, baby."

"Not so good to be awake, ma'am," said Chelsea.

"Better than the alternative, though, yeah?" she said, squeezing the pump of the cuff and checking her watch. She pressed a cold stethoscope to Chelsea's arm. The cuff deflated with a hiss.

"Sound good in there," she said, then looked at Melody. "In here, too. Music's good for this part of the hospital. Wish we had more."

Melody nodded.

"I'm glad it wasn't bothering anyone. I didn't even think

about it, actually. I'm sorry."

"Nothin' to be sorry for," the nurse said. "This is the happiest I've seen some of these patients in days."

"Maybe it's because I'm awake," said Chelsea.

The nurse smiled patiently and patted Chelsea's hand. "I'm sure that's it, baby," she said and strolled from the room, making notes on a clipboard.

Chelsea turned her head weakly to Melody. The two women stared at each other for a long moment.

"Thank you for the music," Chelsea said.

Melody blushed and had no idea what to say. Her eyes filled with tears, and she reached for Chelsea's hand. The woman drew her hand back slightly, and Melody froze.

"You've been nice enough for one day, don't you think?" Chelsea said.

"Just because you have a maximum amount of generosity, doesn't mean everyone does," Phillip said.

Chelsea let her head roll toward him. "Can't I just be bitchy for the first few minutes after I come out of a coma?" she grumbled.

"Not at me," said Melody, finally finding her voice. "You tried to ruin my career, my relationship, and basically my whole new life in New Orleans."

"Didn't do a very good job of it, though, did I?" Chelsea muttered. "You're still here, still playing, and still with Phillip."

Phillip and Melody exchanged a long look over Chelsea's bed. Chelsea's head rocked back and forth between the two of them.

"Oooooh, maybe not, huh? Trouble in paradise?" She laughed, but it was a slurring, drugged laugh rather than a cruel one. Chelsea reached for Phillip and Melody, grabbed an arm each and pulled them closer. "I'm only gonna say this once, and you will never repeat it. You guys are really, really good together."

Her head rolled toward Melody.

"I've never seen him so happy, not even when we first started foolin' around, and I know how to make a man happy. I hate you for that, but almost dying makes me feel generous." Her head rolled toward Phillip. "And you, I don't know what you did that's making her look at you like you're an alligator that ate her puppy off the porch, but you gotta make it right. You were really happy together. What did you do?"

Phillip sighed heavily and locked gazes with Melody. "I didn't believe you, Chelsea," he said.

She began to laugh, then cough, then laugh some more. When the fit subsided, she turned to Melody.

"Oh, honey, don't you know that shows good judgment on his part? I am not always the most honest of women."

"Ain't that the truth," said a deep voice from the doorway. The three of them looked at the man standing there.

"They really gotta turn down this medicine drip," said Chelsea. "I could swear that is Henri LeFontaine darkening my doorway."

"As you live and breathe," said Henri.

"As I live and breathe indeed," said Chelsea thickly.

Henri walked into the room. The electricity between him and Chelsea was palpable. Melody slid her chair away from them and stood next to Phillip. They watched Chelsea and Henri look at one another for a few long moments. Melody realized she'd wrapped her hand in Phillip's, entwining their fingers. Her mind told her to let go of his hand, to let go of her life here in this foreign city, but she didn't.

She drank in his sharp features like a glass of tart fizzing gin and tonic, so tangy and painfully bitter and just a little sweet. Her heart ached for him.

He turned to her. He smiled, hesitantly, his anxiety doing nothing to quell the dimples in his cheeks.

Melody just looked at him, as if for the first time, and fell in love with him all over again. His unshaven jaw made him look rugged. On anyone else, it might have given them an air of rebellion, of danger. On Phillip, she saw the exhaustion and sadness behind it. How would she ever be able to trust him again?

Henri bent toward Chelsea and gave her a quick, gentle peck on the cheek.

"I never thought I'd see you again," she whispered.

"I never thought you'd come out of that coma," he replied. He ran his hand along her cheek, and she closed her eyes in pleasure.

"I'm sorry, Henri. You're the only one I ever really loved. I'm sorry for lying to you, and I'm sorry . . ."

"I'm sorry I left you, baby. It was the biggest mistake I ever made. All these years I regretted it."

Chelsea lifted her hand to his cheek and drew his face toward hers. She couldn't sit up, so he leaned in as far as he could. They kissed, gently, with so much emotion behind it, it charged the air in the room.

As if drawn together magnetically, Phillip and Melody stared at each other. Melody felt like a hundred years passed.

"I want us to work," said Phillip.

"How? How can I believe that you're telling me the whole truth this time?" said Melody, tears pouring down her cheeks.

Phillip held her shoulders gently. "If I could just show you what's in my heart . . ." he said. The sentence trailed off, unfinished.

Henri cleared his throat. He was holding Chelsea's hand in his as if he'd never let it go again. "I do believe I may have a solution to that particular problem."

Chapter Twenty-four

Phillip sat on the exam table, a tangle of wires dangling from the electrodes adhered to his chest. Melody sat in a chair across the room, and a medical technician was begrudgingly attacking the keyboard of some computer equipment with furious typing.

"All set, boss," he said.

Henri nodded. "Thank you, Will, that will be all," he said.

The tech slunk toward the door. He looked unhappily at the trio. He glanced at Henri and waggled a finger at him. "I wasn't here."

"Of course not, Will," he laughed. "This is just a routine equipment check."

Will pursed his lips and looked thoroughly unconvinced but left them alone.

"What is all this again?" asked Melody.

"It's the most advanced EKG machine in the western hemisphere," said Henri, fiddling with some settings on the computer. "It measures the heart rate variability, pulse, and electricity in the patient's heart through transdermal neuro . . . well, let's just say it's really advanced."

"Why are we here?" she asked.

"You, my dear, are going to ask Phillip anything you want to know."

"It's like a lie detector?" she said.

"Kind of, but a more advanced and realistic reading of what's happening in his heart. You did say you wanted to know what was in his heart, yeah? Well, you can lie with your words, but you can't lie with your body."

Melody looked at Phillip, who seemed a little nervous and very uncomfortable in the fluorescent glare of the hospital's overhead lights. He fidgeted slightly, but his gaze never wavered from Melody's face. "Anything you want to know," he said.

Melody stared at him. *Anything.* Her brain swam with the possibilities.

"We have to start with a baseline, of course," said Henri. "What's your name?"

"Phillip Masters."

Henri looked at a scroll of paper being spat out by the tiny printer next to the machine. "Where were you born?"

"Mars," Phillip said, smiling for the first time in what felt like a very long time.

Henri watched the paper, then nodded. "Okay, Melody, we've got a baseline. Ask away."

She paused, considered carefully. *Will you ever hurt me? Can you promise me you'll love me forever? Can you swear to me that you are really a good man?*

"Did you ever love me?"

"Yes," he said. The paper looked identical to the readout when he'd given his name.

"Were you in love with Chelsea?" she asked.

"No," he said emphatically. The stylus skittered across the paper as it had when he'd said the truth. She felt a huge wave of relief wash over her.

"Don't tell *her* that," muttered Henri. "She'd kill ya."

"Do you want to be with me?" Melody could barely get the words out. Her throat felt tight, and her eyes burned.

"Yes," he answered without hesitation. "I want to be with you now, and I want us to stay together for as long as we can, maybe our whole lives. I love you, Melody Bell, and I will never lie to you again. I will tell you the truth, no matter what. I would do anything for you, and if you will take me back, I'll spend my entire life trying to make this up to you."

He paused before continuing. "I loved you from the moment you ran into me, that very first day of auditions, and I will love you for the rest of my days."

Melody's heart beat furiously. She didn't need a readout to tell her that statement was true. Her cheeks were crimson, and a flood of emotion overwhelmed her. She groped around in her mind for some question to lighten the mood.

"What's your second instrument?" she asked. "Besides the violin."

"The trumpet," he answered, without hesitation. "This is the first time I've told anyone what the second instrument I worked so hard to master under Miretti. You're the third person to know," he told her without skipping a beat. He looked at Henri. "Please keep that between us," he said.

Henri shrugged and nodded. "You music folks're strange about what secrets you keep," he said.

Phillip smiled, but Melody's face was still drawn. "Would you have stayed with Chelsea if she had been pregnant?"

Phillip stayed silent for a moment. "I wouldn't have stayed with her, but I would have been a part of that child's life. Chelsea and I were no good together, even casually, but I respect her enough to think she'd have put a kid's needs before her own."

Henri chuckled. "She tried the ol' 'I'm pregnant' trick with you too, then?"

Melody scowled. "It's not very funny, I'd say," she muttered.

"Oh, you gonna have to relax a bit if you gonna stay in N'awlins," drawled Henri.

Melody got a distinct impression that was his true voice, and his doctor's speech was an affectation.

"I would never leave an obligation," said Phillip. "If you'll have me, I will never, ever leave your side. Not out of obligation, but because I love you, and I respect you, and I cannot imagine a life without you."

Henri looked at the paper. "All true, cher. Looks like you've got a decision to make."

She hadn't taken her focus off of Phillip. The plane of his chest, every curve of his muscles, the warmth of his eyes, and the angle of his jaw, she drank it in. She stood and slowly walked across the room. She ran her fingers through his warm, soft hair. She drew her thumb across his stubbly chin and reveled in the scratchiness.

"There's no decision to make," she said. "I'm his, and he is mine."

She kissed him, and Henri watched the machine spit forth rolls of jittery electrified waves on the paper. There was a beat, with skittering jolts of electricity punctuating the rhythm. "Now that's what love looks like, in the heart. It's like a piece of music."

EPILOGUE

A cheerful tune rang through the hallways of the neurology ward at St. Mary's Hospital. Two trumpets played a cheerful duet, their notes chasing each other down the corridors. The nurses tapped their toes, and the energy of the ward changed instantly.

"Must be Tuesday," said Lois, an orderly.

"Sure is," said Francine, the charge nurse. The two women grinned at each other. The music got louder, and as the volume rose, a pair of figures rounded the corner at the end of the corridor.

Melody and Phillip strutted along, popping into and out of rooms with an unsinkable cheer. Some of the patients clapped along with the music. Even those who weren't able to clap nodded along or merely smiled. Everyone was thrilled by the upbeat brass. By the time they worked their way to the nurse's station, they were trailed by a few patients and cheered on by patients and patients' families alike. Francine clapped along from her chair behind the station, grinning. Melody and Phillip finished their song, wailing the final note like it was the last note they'd ever play. They pulled their horns away from their faces with twin flourishes and reveled in the applause. Melody leaned her shoulder into Phillip, and he threw his arm around her. He kissed the top of her head. She thought her heart might burst. New Orleans might not have proved to be the Big Easy for her, but it was worth the effort. Standing there, surrounded by people thrilled and helped by music, she felt like the good times had only just begun to roll.

The End

YOU MAY ALSO ENJOY THE FOLLOWING FROM EXTASY BOOKS INC:

Cult
Seelie Kay

Excerpt

Hope Ali stopped in front of the clothing boutique and pretended to study the ugly dress on the mannequin in the window.

Just outside of her peripheral vision, there was a quick flash of movement. Then it disappeared. Hope frowned. Patience, girl. Patience. Make him come to you. She continued to study the reflections in the window. There. The man in the black jeans and the Bucky Badger hoodie. He had been following her since she left the University of Wisconsin-Madison food court. While she knew Warren Hazelton, her bodyguard, had her within his sights, Hope had convinced him to fall back so she appeared to be alone. It had been a week since the man had begun following her. Today, she was bait. Hope wanted some answers.

Hope didn't know if she had an admirer, a stalker, or someone who had put a target on her back. She didn't really care. The man had pursued her long enough and she wanted it to end. It was the only way she could focus on what was important — getting her degree.

Unfortunately, past experience had taught Hope that she could never be too careful. Her parents were International Law attorneys who fought for the victims of terrorism. Her father, Sheikh Harun Ali, and her mother, Marianne Benson, were fearless and feared. They also had a price on their heads. The year prior, a terrorist posed as a high school student to get close to Hope with the intent of murdering her parents. Hope had almost become collateral damage.

She had fought hard to leave her well-secured family farm outside Milwaukee and attend college in Madison. After all, before she arrived in the United States, she had been educated at British boarding schools. She knew how to survive on her own. Her parents had finally relented when she agreed to round-the-clock surveillance. It was only for a year, after all. Hope had completed most of her college credits through high school Advanced Placement courses and online study during the summer. She'd have her degree in international relations by spring. Then she intended to disappear into the world of international espionage. *If the Agency cuts me some slack.*

Slowly, Hope stepped away from the store window and feigned disinterest. Her gaze remained on the window as she watched the man draw closer. Suddenly, she spun around and ran directly at the man. When she reached him, she swung her right leg and batted the man's legs out from under him. He fell and Hope slammed her high-heeled boot onto his chest. Bucky Badger — the University of Wisconsin mascot on his sweatshirt — appeared none too pleased.

Hope bent over and removed the man's wallet. In her cultured British accent, she crooned, "Hey, baby, perhaps you'd like to tell me why you've been tailing me? I know it's not because of my magnificent ass, though I couldn't blame you if it was." She flipped open the man's wallet and frowned. "Bloody hell! Why the heck is the Secret Service following me?"

The man groaned as Hope removed her boot from his chest

and yanked the man to his feet. He was a little over six feet and lean. She gave him a stink eye and the man shifted uncomfortably. She held out her hand. "Weapon?"

"I can't—"

"You can if you don't want me calling the President and reporting that a nineteen-year-old college student, a foot shorter than you and half your weight, took you down. I suggest you cooperate. Now, hand over your gun or my bodyguard will search all of your . . .private parts. Thoroughly." Hope smirked.

Hazelton, a six-foot-four-inch former U.S. Navy Seal, appeared and pushed a pistol into the man's back. He laughed, a low evil laugh. "Wait until your buddies find out that you were taken down by a teeny, tiny woman. Geesh, where'd you train? Quantico?" His sharp blue eyes crinkled in amusement. He reached under the man's hoodie and removed a gun from his waistband. Hazelton made sure the safety was on and then handed it to Hope.

Hope took the weapon, shoved it into the back of her jean shorts, and adjusted her sweatshirt to cover it. Then she began to tap her foot. "All right, asshole. Explain why you've been following me."

The man flushed. "Damn you, Hazelton, put that gun down." He brushed his dirty blonde hair out of his brown eyes and studied Hope.

Hazelton kept the gun at the man's back. "What's the name on the Secret Service I.D.?"

Hope opened the wallet and studied it. "Daniel J. Perkins."

Hazelton withdrew his gun and placed it in his holster. He began to laugh. "Pesky Perky? No way." He spun the man around and studied him. "Shit, Pesky, you've been working out." Hazelton scowled. "Now why the hell are you following Hope?"

Perkins sighed. "The Ambassador sent me. Cookie Creighton is looking for a roommate. Hope was suggested. I was ordered to check her out, make sure it was safe to place the Ambassador's daughter with her."

"The U.N. Ambassador? Lydia Creighton?" Hope smiled. "She and my mom are friends. I met her last year. That hijacked plane she was on wound up buried in the cornfield next to our farm." She frowned. "Why would she be worried about me? She was right there when I took down one of the hijackers."

"Exactly. The Ambassador wanted to make sure that you don't attract trouble." Perkins shook his head. "Cookie has had problems staying on the straight and narrow. She was booted from her last two colleges. The Ambassador wasn't sure whether you'd be a good or bad influence." He glared at Hazelton. "However, since you hang out with a bunch of thugs, I decided a little reconnaissance was in order."

Hope giggled and nudged Hazelton with her hip. "Did you just call Hazelton a thug? He's been my personal bodyguard since I was sixteen. He's the best, except when he chases away a boy who's interested in me." She smiled. "He's a little over-protective."

Hazelton smirked. "This from the girl who kissed a terrorist last year."

"I didn't know he was a terrorist." Hope slapped at him. "And I didn't know he planned to shoot up my school. At least when he made his move, I got everyone out of my class-room alive."

Perkins gazed at Hazelton, then Hope. He sighed. "That's kind of what the Ambassador was concerned about."

"Oh, shut it, man. The woman is nineteen and smart enough to have skipped from high school straight to her senior year in college. And as you just learned, for a squirt, she is quite capable of protecting herself. Cookie could not have a better roommate." He frowned. "The only question is whether Cookie is good enough for her? I don't want Hope stuck with some loser she constantly has to bail out of trouble. She needs to stay out of the limelight for her own protection. You are aware of who her parents are?"

Perkins nodded. "Sheikh Harun Ali and his wife, Marianne Benson. Do you think Hope is still a target?"

"Not as far as I can tell. She's registered under a false name and has round-the-clock protection. Her building and her apartment are under surveillance twenty-four seven, plus she has a conceal carry permit and a black belt in several martial arts. Cookie couldn't be safer. Again, my worry is who she might bring to the party. The woman sounds like she might need a nanny." He scowled. "How old is she, anyway?"

Perkins frowned. "Twenty-two, but she's only a sophomore, due to all that flunking out."

Hazelton glared at the man. "You want to put a twenty-two-old dimwit in with Hope? Are you crazy?"

"She's not a dimwit. She has an I.Q. of 140. She just gets easily distracted by parties, booze, and men."

"Oh great, a nympho and a drunk. The answer is no." Hazelton scowled. "I am not subjecting Hope to that."

"Guys, I am right here. This is my decision, not yours. I don't have to accept any roommate I don't want." She smiled slightly. "However, it might be nice to have someone else to talk to, other than a bunch of former Seals and Special Forces types."

Perkins sighed. "Will you meet her, then? She has messed up in the past, but she seems determined to make this work. She has no choice. The Ambassador has reached the end of her rope. If she and Bucky Badger don't click, the Ambassador is going to cut her off."

Hope nodded. "I'll meet her for coffee. See what's what. But Hazelton is coming along." She pointed at Perkins. "And tell Cookie, she's buying."

ABOUT THE AUTHOR

Marie Howard grew up on a farm in the Midwest and currently resides in Los Angeles.